Beau Blackstone

Beau Blackstone

Richard Falkirk

All Rights Reserved

Copyright © Richard Falkirk 1973, 2017

First published in 1973 by Eyre Methuen

This edition published in 2017 by:

Thistle Publishing
36 Great Smith Street
London
SW1P 3BU

www.thistlepublishing.co.uk

Author's Note

Of the many books I read during the research for this novel I feel I must single out Terry Coleman's *The Railway Navvies,* published by Hutchinson. It was this fine book which made me appreciate the full potential of my background. I am also particularly indebted to L.T.C. Rolt for *George and Robert Stephenson – The Railway Revolution,* published by Longman, and to Brian Reed for his *Locomotion,* in the Loco Profile series published by Profile Publications Ltd.

Any inaccuracies are mine, not theirs. One, however, is deliberate: Stephenson's "Locomotion" was christened after the period of this narrative, but the old engine is so famous that it would be churlish to leave her in anonymity.

Plan One
The Train Robbery

Chapter One

The highwayman waited in a copse near the Fighting Cocks tavern alternately stroking his horse's neck and fondling the butt of his horse pistol.

He consulted his pocket-watch; three minutes to midnight, three minutes before the stagecoach was due.

The August night was warm but frosted with moonlight, like a rich red wine that has been mistakenly chilled. Leaves rustled above him and in the distance he could see the gleam of the new railway. Even farther away, in the direction of Stockton, there was a glow in the sky from the lamps of the navvies working on the last embankments.

The highwayman talked to his horse. "Not much longer now." The horse pawed the ground impatiently.

The highwayman wore a cloak despite the mild night, a tall hat with a contemptuous brim, and a mask which exaggerated the glitter of his eyes.

Two minutes to go. The rumble of an explosion reached him from the railway workings: the navvies blasting rock, angering the landowners – and their labourers who had been told that the new steam locomotives would make their wives miscarry and their cows run dry. But tomorrow it was the navvies who would be dry because the highwayman was about to steal their wage packets, their beer money.

As the explosion died the highwayman heard the thud of horses' hooves. He consulted his watch again. One minute to midnight. He nodded approvingly because punctuality was the principal accomplice of the criminal. According to his information, which was always good, the driver would be armed with two pistols, his mate with a blunderbuss, a fair defence against the usual highway robbery but not against this one.

An owl hooted and the stagecoach appeared to the highwayman's left, the horses under the whip, as if the driver sensed predators, which wasn't surprising with the gallows down the road where, five years earlier, they had hanged a highwayman.

The highwayman gripped the horse with his thighs and cocked his long-barrelled pistol.

Two hundred yards away his accomplice made his move. He galloped towards the coach, cloak flying, pistol raised, a dark muscle of speed in the silver light.

The highwayman heard the crack of the whip across the coach-horses' backs and the shouts of the driver and his mate. He noticed the shocked faces of the coach's occupants and saw the blunderbuss raised. The explosion filled the countryside with daylight, the spent shot sounding like a summer shower. The highwayman smiled, a rare phenomenon.

His accomplice faltered. The driver took aim with his pistol and fired. The ball clattered into the copse. The accomplice swerved away from the coach and galloped off towards the railway.

The coach slowed down and stopped. The highwayman heard the murmur of voices and laughter hysterical with relief. He whispered to his horse and they trotted towards the quarry waiting for them in the moonlight.

The driver and his mate were standing at the open door of the coach, heady with victory, accepting congratulations, anticipating their reward.

The highwayman spurred his horse and shouted: "Don't move."

For a moment all movement was frozen. Then the driver went for his second pistol. A brave man, thought the highwayman, and a dead one. The bullet hit the driver in the chest, throwing him against the side of the coach. He slid into a sitting position, blood spilling over his clothes.

"And that goes for you, culley," the highwayman said to the driver's mate. "One move from you and you'll be joining your partner." He dismounted and searched him for weapons. Nothing. "Who have you got inside?"

"Three men and a lady." His voice was flaky with fear.

The highwayman peered into the coach without much interest because lifting wallets and watches and jewellery wasn't his style. "Just a friendly warning," he told them. "Don't try anything or I'll blow your heads off."

He turned to the driver's mate. "Where's the swag?"

"What swag?"

The highwayman prodded him with the barrel of the pistol. "Get it." He pointed inside the coach. "I presume two of these gentlemen are puffing Billies from the Stockton and Darlington?"

The driver's mate nodded, his voice a prisoner.

"In charge of the blunt?"

A single word escaped. "Aye."

"Then get it, culley."

The driver's mate climbed up to his seat. The highwayman guessed he was contemplating the other guns under the seat beside the leather bag filled with bank notes and gold sovereigns. "Don't," he advised him, because one killing was enough for a very ordinary job. "Just throw the bag down."

The bag fell heavily, chinking with wealth. The highwayman turned to the pale faces suspended inside the coach. "And now, Billy boys, you'll have to move quickly because the navvies are planning to go on the randy this weekend and if they don't get their wages God help the S and D. God help everyone within ten miles of it," he added reflectively. He peered at the two railwaymen, seeing middle-class comfort which was something he despised more than aristocratic idleness. Hatred sharpened his voice. "And God help you two gentlemen if the navvies ever suspect you lifted their blunt."

He walked back to his horse, limping slightly, remounted, fired the remaining barrel of his pistol at the incurious stars and galloped away. The shot made the horses move and, as the coach inched forward, the body of the driver fell back on the roadside.

A mile down the road the highwayman reined his horse to check the contents of the bag. Two thousand pounds including the money to pay contractors and engineers. A fair enough purse. But highway robbery for a criminal of his calibre? The highwayman shrugged, consoling himself with the knowledge that soon it would be his privilege to carry out the world's first train robbery.

He took his payment of £100 in notes from the bag; and, because there had been a killing, helped himself to a £50 bonus. Then he strapped the bag to the saddle and turned the horse's head towards Darlington, galloping past the gallows at great speed.

Three weeks later in an inn called The Naked Man, twenty miles from the scene of the highway robbery, a man dressed with care and amusement.

He took off a grey, swallow-tail coat, royal blue waistcoat and breeches made by Weston, the Old Bond Street tailor who had dressed Beau Brummel, and soft leather boots by Hoby, the Duke of Wellington's bootmaker. He folded the clothes carefully, put them in a trunk, and stood for a moment in the middle of the low-beamed room, naked and not unlike the figure in the inn sign. His body was powerful although the skin was delicate in places with scar tissue. He had the thighs of a horseman, the shoulders of a sedan-chair carrier and the face of a poetical prizefighter.

He put away his guns with his discarded clothes. A Manton pocket pistol, a Perry conversion of a 1790 flintlock and a couple of duelling pistols by Outridge snug in their baize-lined case beside powder flask, bullet mould, balls, cleaning rod and turn-screw. He was left with a battered flintlock with rust on the barrel which he handled with distaste. When he cocked it the sound was like an old man kneeling.

Then he began to dress: moleskin trousers, double-canvas shirt, velveteen coat, hobnail boots, sealskin cap which had cost him £1 5s more than it was worth – red silk handkerchief with white spots round his neck and a waistcoat which embraced most of the spectrum.

He examined himself in a long, tarnished mirror which made no contribution to narcissism, and grinned. He took off the rainbow waistcoat and the sealskin cap because they were for special occasions such as pay-day brawls.

Then he went down the drunken stairs, winked at the landlord whom he had bribed to keep quiet and walked out into the purring summer day to buy the rest of his gear – a bag, a shovel and a dog.

He got the bag for 3*d*, the shovel for 2*s*, and the dog for 1*d*, which was more than it was worth. It had a ratty face, reddish eyes, a nature that responded only to the boot and a short, upright, immobile tail. He called it Wagger.

When he returned to the inn he sat down at a table and ordered himself a dog's nose because it seemed appropriate.

The landlord, a jovial and mean man, sat down opposite him. "I suppose," he said, "I'm not allowed to know what this is all about."

Edmund Blackstone, Bow Street Runner, took the rusty pistol from his belt. "You suppose correctly," he said. "And should you try to find out – should you as much as lay a finger on my trunk upstairs. ..."

He cocked the pistol and together they listened to its knee-joint crack.

After his second dog's nose he went outside and, accompanied by his dog, attended to himself. He poured ale over his clothes, and rubbed his fingernails against the stone wall of The Naked Man until they were cracked and jagged. Then he dishevelled his hair, rubbing a little grease into it. The whole process offended him but he persevered, massaging soil into his hands until they had a dirty polish about them. He also applied a little dirt to his face, feeling a day's growth of stubble rasp under his fingers.

What else? His hobnail boots looked too new so he scuffed them in the dust. The dog stared at the boots, sizing up the enemy. What else? Blackstone's hands still bothered him because they didn't have the saddle-hard palms which you got wielding a shovel for twelve or more hours a day, but there wasn't much more he could do about them. Nor was there much more he could do about the styling of his hair, except attack it with a pair of scissors. He considered this and rejected it, wondering if he was making a mistake. He had made several recently and one more wouldn't surprise him; but still he didn't take the scissors to his hair – there were limits.

He knelt and examined the dog. It had a scarred muzzle and herring-bone ribs and exuded hatred; but when it curled its lip, which was often, its teeth were sharp and white. Blackstone fetched it some sausages. It swallowed them whole, reminding Blackstone of a snake swallowing small animals whole. After the meal the dog regarded him guardedly, thumb-sized tail unmoving. Then man and dog returned to the tavern looking as if they belonged to each other.

The girl had been crying and one eye was badly bruised. She was standing at the bar, plump breasts pushed against the woodwork. Blackstone sat down, ordered himself a pot of ale and listened.

"Just a little bread," the girl said. "And some ale. Surely you can spare that." Her face was ghosted with exhaustion.

"Let's see the colour of your money first," the landlord said. He was polishing glasses, lamplight gleaming on his jolly face. He grinned at Blackstone and winked. "Or had you some other sort of payment in mind?"

The girl sagged against the bar.

The landlord said: "You can't come into a tavern without a penny in your pocket and expect victuals." He held a glass up to the light and hung it above the bar. "Where have you come from? Shanty Town?"

The girl nodded. "I can't go much farther."

Her voice had London edges to it. The voice of the slums, the rookeries. Blackstone put her age at seventeen. But you couldn't tell. Sixteen, eighteen – she would be finished by the time she was twenty.

Blackstone said: "Give her some food and ale."

The landlord's hands froze on a tankard. His eyes set in cherubic flesh were bright blue. He hadn't resented taking orders from the elegant stranger who had arrived that morning with sovereigns jingling in his pockets; not even from the flamboyant navvy who had reappeared, because there was still an air of authority about him; but not from this unkempt moucher who had returned from the courtyard with his snapping mongrel. "Who says so?" he asked.

Blackstone considered his position. Navvies seeking employment on the Stockton and Darlington Railway didn't issue commands imperious with Bow Street authority. You didn't destroy your cover with the first harlot you met – a navvies' harlot at that; the mistakes had to stop some time.

The girl turned. "Yes," she said, "who says so?" She appraised Blackstone. "An out-of-work navigator? Come off it, my covey."

Blackstone searched the pockets of his velveteen coat. "I'll tell you what I'll do. I was going to have some bread and cheese. I'll share it with you."

She shook her head. "I'd rather dab it up with him." She pointed contemptuously at the landlord.

Blackstone sighed. What was one more mistake? He tossed two shillings on the bar. "Get her some victuals."

The girl threw the coins back at him. "Charity from a navvy? Not on your bloody life. I'd rather...."

But they had no way of knowing what she would rather do because she slid to the ground unconscious.

The landlord came round the bar and Blackstone said: "Keep your hands off her." He felt the girl's pulse; it was steady enough so he picked her up and laid her on a leather-padded bench beside the unlit fire. "Now get some food," he told the landlord.

When she came round there was cold mutton and bread and pickles in front of her and some gin and hot water. Her pride hadn't re-awoken and she ate ravenously. Blackstone poured hot water into the gin and pushed the glass across the table. She tossed the drink back, shuddered and stared at him resentfully.

Her face was pretty in a sulky sort of way; the sort of looks described as sluttish by those who don't know that sluttishness is an enforced occupation in the rookeries, preferable to skivvying or scrubbing doorsteps on raw knees. Her hair was reddish with a few ringlets still uncurled; her mouth was petulant and needed a smile; her pushed-up breasts were still firm.

After a few more moments of resentment she said: "Thanks." Her tone had little connection with gratitude. "And now what do you want?"

"Nothing."

"A navvy wanting nothing? Do me a favour."

"What's your name?"

"Dolly. Molly. Polly. Take your pick."

"Molly," Blackstone said. "Where are you from?"

"You ask a lot of questions." She poured herself more gin and stared at him suspiciously. "Where do you come from?"

"The same place as you, I think. A long way from here. London. Holborn. The St Giles Rookery. Am I right?"

She relaxed a little. "You could be. I was born in a basement overlooking a dung heap."

"Ah," Blackstone said. "I remember that dung heap – we're neighbours."

She almost smiled. "Are you going to work on the S and D?"

Blackstone nodded.

"Don't bother, culley. Get back to the canals." She leaned across the table showing a lot of her breasts. "But there's something about you. You don't look as if you and hard work are partners."

Which was the trend these days, Blackstone reflected. Within five minutes of meeting a navvies' tallywoman she had spotted a flaw. Already the assignment had the familiar feel of failure about it.

First there had been the case of the Barbican swindler. Blackstone had chased him across the English Channel to Havre de Gras, always one step behind, then lost him. Blackstone was not ashamed of his efforts: Sir Richard Birnie, the Bow Street Magistrate, was. The penman had cashed a forged cheque for £400 and got away in a hackney carriage. One hackney to be traced among the hundreds in London. Blackstone asked Glindons to print handbills offering a reward to the driver and a man known as Boss-eyed Jack came forward. He said he had taken the penman to a flash tavern in Clements Lane. From there Blackstone traced him to the George Inn at Crawley, to Brighton where he had bought a gold watch for £35, to the Marine Hotel at Worthing; then Arundel, Chichester, Havant and the Red Lion at Fareham. Finally to Wheelers Hotel at Havre de Gras. Blackstone arrived just as the ship taking his quarry to New York cast off. "I only just missed him," he told Birnie. "But you missed him," Birnie replied.

Then there had been the duel between two powdered aristocrats. Full of brandy and bravado the night before, they met at dawn the next day, palsied with fear. They aimed wavering pistols at each other, fired and missed and Blackstone didn't bother to take any action. They reported him to Birnie for failing to report them and Birnie said, "Two failures in a row."

They usually came in threes.

"When did you last do any hard work?" the girl asked.

"Never you mind," said Blackstone, awaiting the inspiration which had deserted him lately. It came to him, sluggishly. "You should see my hams," he said.

She looked at him mystified.

"You haven't been on the treadmill. You don't know what it does to your legs. It doesn't affect your hands." He showed her his dirty palms. "It's your legs that the treadmill fixes."

Her expression softened. "You've been inside?"

"The House of Correction," Blackstone told her.

"If you're on the run," she said, "take my advice – go to the canals. That's where the security is. There's only a couple of months' work left on this bloody railway. And you'll have to put up with Petro."

"Petro?" Blackstone asked. "Who's Petro?" Although he knew.

"Calls himself king of the navvies. A bastard," she added. "Don't cross him. ... What's your name, by the way?"

"Whitestone," Blackstone told her.

"You won't be for long. They'll give you another handle." She smiled for the first time, banishing the sulkiness, and Blackstone saw what she might have been. "Let's think of one." She studied him. "You come from St Giles Rookery – how about Rookie?"

"Rookie it is," Blackstone said. "But I'll give the canals a miss for the time being – too much like hard work when you've just done time. I'll toughen myself up on the S and D."

A reasonable argument, Blackstone decided, remembering that canal navvies dug the equivalent of a 36-foot-long trench three feet deep and three feet wide every day; remembering the men entombed by falls of earth and rock, the men killed by explosions, maimed by breakaway loads crashing down barrow runs on the cuttings, men frozen in winter or knocked out with heat exhaustion in the summer. Remembering the camp-followers – cholera, dysentery, smallpox and typhus. All for a few shillings a day. The scourge of the countryside, they were called when they rioted or went on the randy. Who was to blame them?

Blackstone said: "Tell me more about Petro."

"You'll find out soon enough."

"Why are you so scared of him?"

The friendliness faded a little. "Everyone's scared of him. Even the contractors. He's never lost a fight and he's got four bodyguards. Every pay-day the navvies have to pay him a penny. If they don't they get beaten up. One died once," she said. "And another lost an eye."

Blackstone began to look forward to meeting the king of the navvies. "Does he have an excuse for taking their money?"

"He claims it's funds for a society to protect the navvies. To get fair wages and decent food at the tommy shops instead of rotten meat and watered ale."

"That sounds fair enough."

"Lining the pockets of Petro – that's the only fund that gets any richer."

Blackstone walked around the parlour. They were the only customers; they and the dog which trailed him, curling its lip at invisible rats. It was dark outside and the summer sky was lazy with stars. Blackstone contemplated the stars for a moment with foreboding: he felt he was about to make another mistake.

When he returned to the table the girl was pouring herself more gin. Gently, he took it away from her. "Not in your condition," he said. "You're exhausted. Where are you heading for?"

She told him she was going to London; that she was sick of being a navvies' tallywoman.

"London's a long way," Blackstone said. "Two hundred miles or so. How are you going to get there without any brass?"

The sulkiness returned. "The usual way."

"How old are you?"

"It's none of your bloody business. Just because you bought me some victuals it doesn't mean you have any rights."

"I don't want any rights."

Suddenly she took one of his hands, examining the palm. "Strong," she said. "But soft as a baby's. Take a tip – rub them with meths or they'll be raw meat within a couple of days."

Blackstone then made three mistakes because, like failures, that was the way they came. First he took her upstairs and told her to use his bed for the night. Then, while she was feeling the sheets which were almost clean, he slipped a sovereign into her pocket.

The third mistake was perpetrated in the courtyard. The stars were deep in the sky and the air smelled of wet hay. Her scent reminded him of honeysuckle, of the brevity of summer and the brevity of lives seeded in the rookeries. He kissed her and felt her lips part; she clung to him for a moment.

Then he was gone, with the dog trotting behind him like a spectre of failure.

Chapter Two

The briefing had been held in the fine Gothic home of Sir Joshua Eccleston near the 24-mile-long Stockton and Darlington Railway in the north-east of England. Present: Sir Joshua, merchant banker, luminary and railway baron of the future; Sir Richard Birnie, one-time saddlemaker, favourite of George IV and Chief Bow Street Magistrate; Edmund Blackstone, Bow Street Runner.

"I'm honoured," said Sir Joshua in his after-dinner voice, "that you gentlemen have thought fit to come here three weeks after we sought your help." He crossed his legs and folded his hands across his neat, plump belly; his zealous bishop's face was rosy with indignation.

Birnie lit his churchwarden pipe and blew foul smoke across the tea-table on the terrace. The garden was drowsy with summer; the herbaceous border clotted with blossom, the shaved lawns alive with sparrows. A maid in a black uniform hovered nearby.

Sir Joshua stared across the Spode tea-set and the plate of Sally Lunn cakes as if the ladies had retired after dinner and the port was circulating. "Very honoured," he went on, his voice gaining power, "that you have at last realized the danger to the world's first public steam locomotive railway."

Birnie waved the smoke-dribbling stem of his pipe. "I think you exaggerate a little, Sir Joshua. There has, after all, been only one highway robbery. My men are employed on rather more important matters. Like guarding the King," he added.

"The protection of the Stockton and Darlington is surely of some importance?"

"Agreed. That's why I've come personally and brought one of my best men with me." He stared through Blackstone, whom he had recently accused of negligence.

"But you've left it late. The next stagecoach carrying wages leaves in a couple of days. However" – his voice was mollified – "it is an honour for the Bow Street Magistrate himself to come personally."

Blackstone said: "Sir Richard was insistent that he conduct the investigation at first hand."

He took a pinch of Fribourg and Treyer snuff. Birnie had journeyed north only because he shared with Blackstone an interest in steam engines and railways, and before leaving he had warned: "If you fail again, Blackstone, I'll put you back on the foot patrol."

Sir Joshua snapped his fingers and the maid, who was young and pretty, poured more tea.

Birnie said: "You seem to think this is more than just an isolated case of highway robbery, Sir Joshua. May I ask why?"

Eccleston drank his tea with his little finger crooked. "I have information – I believe that's the phrase – that there is a conspiracy afoot."

Blackstone asked: "What kind of a conspiracy?" He placed his gilt-crowned baton on the table to remind himself of his authority.

"A conspiracy among the navvies." Sir Joshua might have been referring to prisoners on the hulks.

"Ah," Blackstone said, "the dangerous classes." It was customary to blame navvies for pillage, murder, rape and riot: now they were highwaymen.

Blackstone's cynicism reached Birnie, who was always suspicious of his sympathies. His bleak, moorland features frowned. He said: "We'll have to be careful. The navvies tend to stick together."

Sir Joshua said: "A conspiracy of silence, you mean?" He liked courtroom clichés.

"Just that," Birnie said.

A tacit rebuke because Blackstone had once encountered such a conspiracy. The murder of a parish constable two years ago. It had started as a commonplace pay-day brawl between the Scots and Irish navigators digging a canal, with the English fighting anyone they could lay their fists on. The Irish destroyed a couple of Scots' shanties and next day the Scots razed the whole Irish settlement. War was declared and the two armies met in a tunnel with the Dragoons, constables and magistrates waiting uncertainly at either end. There was no victory or defeat in the dripping pipeline; but as the armies emerged a pistol was fired and a constable dropped dead. When Blackstone questioned the navvies, enemies became allies and no one talked.

Blackstone said: "Just what sort of a conspiracy, Sir Joshua?"

Sir Joshua took a delicate bite from a Sally Lunn. "According to the information laid, the highway robbery was organized by a number of navvies who have devised a plan to get paid twice. They rob the stagecoach carrying their wages, then threaten to riot if they're not paid immediately."

Birnie said: "And you think they're going to stage another robbery?"

"According to my information," Sir Joshua said.

"Then it shouldn't be difficult to forestall them," Birnie said. "What do you think, Blackstone?"

Blackstone shrugged. "Who was this information laid with?"

"George Stephenson," Sir Joshua told him.

"And he called in Bow Street?"

"Correct."

"A great man," Birnie observed.

And for a moment they were all in agreement.

George Stephenson had started life as a cattle herdsman. By the age of fifteen he was a steam pump fireman at Black Callerton colliery. By seventeen he was learning to read and write. Then he became engine-wright at Killingworth colliery. By the time he was in his early thirties he had built a steam-blast engine which could haul a thirty-ton load at 4mph. Now he was engineer on the S and D and the Liverpool–Manchester – if it ever got built.

On the terrace Sir Joshua was talking about the threat to the railways. But Blackstone knew it all.

The S and D had split the country. The opposition comprised the canal owners who saw their prosperity vanishing on the iron roads and the landowners who saw their pastures being devastated. The landowners' allies were their labourers who had been told that the locomotives would ruin them. Even horses were against the railway, according to a handbill which showed two tin-ribbed nags contemplating an engine over a fence. "Our successor," said one. "Our executioner," said the other.

The railways were supported by industrialists and visionaries such as Sir Joshua Eccleston because they were speed, they were progress, and they would make them more money.

The S and D battle had been won. The first round of the Liverpool–Manchester battle had been lost because of

George Stephenson's evidence before a parliamentary committee. His flinty Northumbrian accents had sounded like a foreign language to the MPs.

Blackstone had read the report containing his evidence:

Q: What is the width of the Irwell there?
A: I cannot say exactly at present.
Q: How many arches is your bridge to have?
A: It is not determined upon.
Q: How could you make an estimate for it then?
A: I have given a sufficient sum for it.

Blackstone sorrowed for the self-made genius who had been threatened with ducking and violence during his surveys; his men had been stoned, but they had pressed on, taking levels at night and firing guns to divert the enemy. Then to be defeated by a lack of sophistication, a dialect – and a certain disregard of detail.

Blackstone looked forward to meeting Stephenson.

The maid poured the last of the tea. It was 4.30. The sun was hotter than ever and sweat trickled down Blackstone's chest. He wished he hadn't worn the royal blue waistcoat.

The scent of blossom was heavy this purring afternoon and he fancied he could smell steam and gunpowder, oil and smoke from the railway.

Sir Joshua said: "It's as simple as this – the highway robberies are a threat to the S and D. If the navvies miss another pay-day they might wreck it. If the S and D fails then the Liverpool–Manchester project will be thrown out again." His voice gathered volume. "Britain will still be idling along on its waterways while the rest of the world takes to steam...."

Blackstone interrupted him. "I believe you have considerable financial interest in the S and D *and* the Liverpool–Manchester, Sir Joshua?"

"I'm investing in Britain's future," Sir Joshua said.

"Very commendable," Birnie said. He was dressed, as usual, in black, an ascetic Scots preacher beside Sir Joshua the bishop.

Blackstone said: "The local opposition was led by Sir Geoffrey Hawkins, wasn't it?"

"A decadent reactionary landowner," Sir Joshua said.

"I'm his guest," Birnie said.

There was a pause during which the murmur of insects sounded loud.

Sir Joshua said: "You astound me. Is he a friend of yours?"

"An acquaintance," Birnie said. "We've had some stimulating arguments about railways in the past."

"He tried to wreck the S and D," Sir Joshua said.

Birnie said: "There's a lot to be said for establishing yourself in the enemy camp."

"Very true," Sir Joshua said. There was a vestige of admiration in his voice.

Birnie went on: "This is what I propose to do. Blackstone will take steps to protect the next consignment of money. He will also operate under cover as a navvy and find out who's behind the plot."

Sir Joshua nodded appreciatively. "It seems quite sound," he said, adding magnanimously, "Edmund Blackstone has quite a reputation."

"Yes," Birnie said grimly, "he has."

Sir Joshua looked zealous. He leaned across the table and asked: "Just how do you propose to stop the next robbery, Mr Blackstone?"

Blackstone said: "I think the blunt – the money – should be taken by a different route on a different day. Say two days later than planned."

"A good idea," Sir Joshua said earnestly. "But make a pretence of loading the money on the usual day?"

"Exactly. And fill it with passengers who know how to shoot straight."

"We mustn't fail," Sir Joshua said. He hesitated. "After this there's only one more delivery of money. A big one."

The sweat cooled on Blackstone's chest. "How big?"

"Something like £10,000 – paying off the navvies, the contractors, the engineers."

If I fail, Blackstone thought, then at least it will be on a spectacular scale. He said: "One thing, Sir Joshua, who was your informant?"

Eccleston looked importantly worried. "Is it all right for me to say?"

"If I don't know the informant's identity then I can't even begin the inquiry."

Eccleston fiddled with the watch-chain looped over his plump stomach. "I thought there was a question of ethics...."

"To hell with ethics," Blackstone snapped. "Who is he?"

"All I can tell you," Eccleston said, "is that he's known as Frying Pan Charlie."

Chapter Three

Frying pan Charlie was difficult to find.

Petro, king of the navvies, was easier: he found Blackstone.

The summons came one hot evening when Blackstone was lying on his bunk in the leaking shed he shared with twenty-five other navvies, a tallywoman, a crone called Alice, a wife in labour, and a few dozen rats. The shed was called The Rectory.

One of Petro's bodyguards, stripped to the waist, with a doormat of hair on his chest and a drum for a belly, pushed open the door, helped himself to a pot of ale guarded by the crone and asked her which was the new man. She pointed at Blackstone.

The bodyguard came over to his bunk. "You the cove they call Rookie?"

Blackstone, lying with bandaged hands behind his neck, said he was.

"Petro wants you."

"Does he?" Blackstone said.

The bodyguard blinked.

Blackstone said conversationally: "What's your name?"

"They call me the Gorger."

"I'm not surprised," Blackstone said, "with tripes like that." He sat up and poked the drum-like belly.

The Gorger pulled him out of the bunk with one hand. "Shut your fly trap," he said. "Or I'll give you a squeeze." He stood back, arms hanging loosely. "There's one or two here who will tell you what happens when I give someone a squeeze, aren't there, lads?" He appealed to the navvies eating their supper, mending their boots, supping ale. "I've cracked a few ribs in The Rectory in my time."

No one answered.

"Haven't I, Fanny Punch?" He addressed a surprisingly small and thin navvy. Fanny Punch said he had.

"Haven't I, Yankee Tom?" A lanky American nodded and spat tobacco juice; he didn't seem overawed by the bodyguard.

Blackstone stared reflectively at the Gorger. Because he was working under cover he had decided not to draw attention to himself. That meant backing down to a fat bully. On the other hand he might gain Petro's respect if he beat the Gorger. This appealed to him most. He clenched his blistered hands.

Yankee Tom said: "I should do as he says if I were you, Rookie."

"You're not me," Blackstone said.

It was quiet in the shed, the men sitting on the tiers of bunks watching, boots and suppers forgotten. At the far end of the shed Alice sat rocking in her chair beside a copper filled with boiling water in which navvies' dinners were suspended like fishing bait on lengths of string – beef, bacon, a freshly-snared rabbit – and two barrels of beer.

Through the open door babies and dogs playing in the evening sunshine.

The Gorger said: "Are you coming?" There was an undertone of uncertainty in his voice.

"In my own time."

The Gorger took a step forward. "You're coming now, my covey."

Blackstone moved to one side; if you got caught in those arms, which were as thick as some men's thighs, you were lost. "Slippy, aren't you," the Gorger said. "Slippy and lippy. I never liked smart London coves anyway." He began to edge Blackstone towards a corner.

Blackstone was glad he still had his hobnail boots on. He moved quickly to the right towards Alice's territory. Her rocking chair creaked rhythmically: she watched them without much interest: she had seen many brawls.

The Gorger closed in and Blackstone kicked him below the knee with the heel of his boot, scraping it down his shin and stamping on his instep. The Gorger bent forward and Blackstone brought his knee into his face. Then he hit him with his left elbow, left fist and right fist. But the Gorger didn't go down; instead he spat out a tooth. "You bastard," he said. Blackstone kicked him on the other leg.

The Gorger backed across the room, grabbed a heavy black saucepan and filled it with boiling water. "This is for your face," he said. "That flash face of yours. No more molls for you, culley, not after this." The rhythm of the rocking chair was unchanged.

Yankee Tom's bunk was in the middle of three tiers. He was lying with his head propped on one hand. He didn't change his position. Merely kicked with his right foot sending the saucepan flying out of the bodyguard's hand.

The Gorger paused, swearing.

Blackstone grabbed the saucepan and cracked him on the head with it. "Fair's fair, culley," he said.

This time the bodyguard fell. He tried to get up but it was only hatred fuelling him. Blackstone put his foot on his throat. "Go back and tell Petro I'll be with him in a minute."

"He'll kill me," the Gorger said.

"I will if you don't do what I tell you."

The bodyguard stood up, hand feeling the swelling on his temple. "Supposing you've broken my skull," he said.

Blackstone shrugged.

"I'll do you for this," the Gorger said. "One dark night I'll do for you."

"I'll be waiting," Blackstone said. "Now get out. I'll watch you over to Petro's hut."

The navvies watched him stumble across the field in the middle of Shanty Town and go into the king's wooden palace.

Blackstone turned to Yankee Tom. "Thanks," he said.

Alice pulled up a joint of bacon from her cauldron. "Your dinner's ready, Rookie," she said.

Blackstone walked slowly across the field. Behind him the sun was setting over the railway embankment which was littered with barrows and tools like discarded toys. He imagined Stephenson's locomotive puffing along the line in a month's time and a familiar exhilaration caught hold of him. Part of progress, evolution. A time for change was upon the land.

Shanty Town sprawled in the lengthening shadow of the embankment. Wooden sheds, sod huts, each with its name – Primrose Cottage, The Cuttings, Somerset House, St James's Palace. Sparks from open fires spiralled into the sky like fireflies while on the balding grass the navvies drank and played cards and the women cooked and breast-fed their babies. At one end of the settlement two navvies were engaged in a shin-kicking contest; with moleskin trousers hitched up to their knees, they took turns to kick; money was staked on each and the one who gave up first lost. At the opposite end of the site the money was going on a dog-fight.

These were the men who had built a railway. They were its sinews; their unmarked graves its sleepers.

Blackstone whistled to his dog; but there was no need – it was behind him on its invisible lead.

He paused outside the palace of the king of the navvies. It was neat by comparison with the patchwork homes around. With a chimney stack and a bright yellow door guarded by two henchmen and a gnarling Staffordshire bull terrier. Blackstone tied up his mongrel a safe distance from the Staffordshire, pushed past the bodyguards and walked in without knocking.

The King sat back in his chair, thumbs in his belt, and appraised Blackstone. On the table in front of him was a pint of gin and a jug of water. His face was tanned and scarred, his freshly-shaven chin still blue with a cleft in it in which you could tuck your little finger. Everything about him was brown and his bright blue eyes were a shock. He wore a single gold ear-ring – the lobe of his other ear had been torn off – and he was smoking a stubby clay pipe.

He had a woman visitor.

Petro said: "You must be the man they call Rookie."

"I understand you wanted to see me."

"I did, Rookie. I did indeed." He wore a Bristol-yellow handkerchief at his neck and his voice had a cidery, West Country richness about it. "My bodyguard tells me you were reluctant to see me?"

Blackstone said: "I wanted to finish my dinner first."

"Did you," said Petro. "Did you indeed." He aimed the stubby pipe like a pistol. "He tells me you got five other navvies to beat him up."

"Do you believe that?"

Petro re-lit his pipe and sucked at it. He shook his head. "Not really," he said. "Not really." He had a habit of repeating himself. He gestured to the girl sitting opposite him. "I want you to meet a woman of God."

Blackstone bowed.

Petro said: "Miss Josephine Courtney. She's a missionary and she's come to reform us poor navvies." He stood up and stretched. "Perhaps we need reforming. What do you think, Rookie?"

"Most people could do with a bit of reforming." Blackstone turned to the girl. "Why don't you start with the owners, ma'am. The contractors. The gangers. Why pick on the navvies?"

She had a determined face, almost pretty, with a mole on her cheek and a few fair ringlets escaping from the sides of her poke bonnet.

She said: "Because, Mr Rookie, the owners and contractors do not go around terrorizing innocent citizens and ruining their own health with drink." She stared at the pint of gin.

Blackstone said: "With respect, ma'am, perhaps you might feel like a wet after twelve hours shovelling earth and rock."

Petro said: "Why have you picked on us, ma'am? There are a lot of *dangerous classes* – apart from us. What about the coasters, the gypsies?"

She had a worn Bible and a bundle of tracts on her knee; she tapped them impatiently. "Because you haven't found God yet."

"There's many that haven't found him. Why pick on the navvies?"

"You don't make time to go to Church. Why, you even work on Sundays," she said accusingly. "Someone must bring God to you."

Petro walked round the room, palatial by shanty standards, papered with newsprint carrying stories of navvy riots and copies of *Hue and Cry,* furnished with a bed, table and chairs, chiming clock, sewing machine, a pair of Indian clubs and a ship's figurehead. He swung one of the clubs lazily and said: "It wouldn't be that the owners want God to keep us in order a bit, would it, so that we get more work done?"

Josephine Courtney said she didn't even know the owners. Nor was she the first missionary to bring God to the navvies. Hadn't they heard of Rev. Richard Thomson, known as Decency Dick, who had preached to the navvies and dropped dead one hot Sunday on the word amen? Navvies had journeyed twenty miles to attend his funeral.

"So we can't be all bad," Petro said.

"No one said you were. But your men must be taught."

Noting the "your men", Blackstone decided that Josephine Courtney was no fool.

"They're their own worst enemies the way they drink," she said.

Petro poured himself some gin, offering the bottle to Blackstone. Blackstone refused. Petro said: "You've got a lot of good work ahead of you this weekend when the men go on the randy. If they're paid, that is," he added.

"If only I could stop them," she said.

"Like stopping the Severn Bore," Petro told her.

Blackstone asked why she was so concerned with drink. "What about our disgusting morals? There's enough been written about them."

The girl spoke tersely. "I know all about the tallywomen. But I can't do anything about it when the men are in drink."

"And the women," Petro said.

"So I thought if I took up the problem of liquor first."

"Nothing wrong with a bit of booze," Petro said. He grinned. "In moderation, of course. Nothing wrong with a drop of lightning." He pointed at the gin.

She turned to Blackstone. "What do you think, Mr Rookie? You don't seem to be a drinking man."

Petro glanced at Blackstone suspiciously. "What's the matter with you anyway? Don't you like to get a bit lushy?"

"On occasions," Blackstone said.

Petro returned to the girl. "Where's your pulpit? Where's your Church? Where are you going to shack up?" He winked at Blackstone. "You can always shack up with me."

"I've got rooms in the village. And the open air is my Church."

"Where do you come from?" Blackstone asked.

"Not far."

"How far?"

"Lancashire," she said vaguely. She stood up. "And now I must be about God's work." She took two tracts from the bundle and gave them to Petro and Blackstone. "There's more than sermons in them," she confided.

The tract was called *The Navigator*, a single sheet folded down the middle. There were many obituaries. Where death was natural or accidental the tone was commiserative; where liquor was the executioner it was reproachful. "Lethro Higgins known as Red Peggy, buried under a fall of earth. A decent man, may God rest his soul." "Tosher Martin, age unknown, died of a bite" – it didn't say who bit him – "welcome to His Kingdom." The author was less charitable about Rummy Roberts who "got drunk and was run over by a coach and four" observing "They do say that Rummy died happy. A false happiness for which he will pay the price in Purgatory."

"Did you write this?" Blackstone asked.

"Some of it."

"And this?" He pointed at a recipe to kill the craving for drink. "Gentian 1 oz, quassia ¼ oz, lemon ¼ oz, ½ gallon of boiling water to be poured over these; bottle it when cold and take half a cupful twice a day."

"No," she said, "that is the recipe of a missionary who works among the under-privileged classes in the rookeries of London."

"Ah," Blackstone said, "the rookeries. Terrible places, ma'am."

Petro said: "Has it occurred to you, Miss Josephine, why they call him Rookie?"

She was unabashed. "I'm sure Mr Rookie will agree that the poor souls who live in the rookeries are under-privileged." She leaned forward in her chair and stared at Blackstone. "As a matter of fact there is something familiar about you."

"Have you ever been to the rookeries, ma'am?"

"I've never even been to London."

"Then you can't have seen me," Blackstone said emphatically, wondering if she had seen him elsewhere.

"I suppose not. It's just. ..."

"Just what, ma'am?"

"I don't know. My imagination, I suppose."

Petro was reading his *Navigator*. "Did you write this?" He read out: "Warning of crimes being committed among navvies." Blackstone detected wariness in his tone.

"That's compiled at headquarters," the girl told him. She stood up and adjusted her bonnet, her halo. "We all send in reports."

Blackstone read the warnings. "Beware two gentlemen known as Cat's Meat and Salt-and-Pepper who were taken off the streets in the throes of drink at Lancaster by their mates and repaid them by 'doing a moonlight', at 3 am, taking with them £2 8s 6d, two pairs of boots, baccy and two pairs of moleskin trousers. If you find these rascals give them what for."

Blackstone laughed. "Is that one of yours?"

"Yes," she said. "What of it?"

"Nothing," he said. "I see there's nothing about swearing in this issue. You missionaries are usually upset by swearing."

"In my opinion," she said, "it's one of the lesser evils."

"I once heard a preacher claim that horses didn't like oaths. They much preferred to be addressed decently, according to him."

"What about dogs?" Petro asked. "They don't seem to mind."

"I don't know about dogs," Josephine Courtney said. "Now I must be off. But please remember, Mr Petro, that I'm relying on you. If I have your support then I can win them round." She peered out of the window where two men were still kicking each other's shins in the firelight. "Well some of them, anyway." She smiled at Petro, dimpling a little. "Where you lead, Mr Petro, they will follow."

Petro looked pleased. "Don't expect too much," he said.

"I won't." She turned to Blackstone. "I look forward to making your acquaintance again, Mr Rookie." She frowned. "I could have sworn that we've met somewhere before."

"I don't think so, ma'am."

Petro opened the door for her. Outside the wooden cottage the bull terrier and Blackstone's mongrel faced each other. Petro told a bodyguard to escort her back to the village.

She smiled. "Thank you. Thank you both. May God be with you."

Petro closed the door. "He'd better be with you, culley," he said.

Once they had called him Gypsy because of his dark looks, his ear-ring and his swift, knife-edged ways. Peter the Gypsy. But he had objected, finding an insult in the Romany implication. He had fought and beaten anyone calling him Gypsy so they had called him Petro, which had a gypsy ring about it, a compromise.

He sat at the table and lit his stubby pipe. "Just who the hell do you think you are?" he asked.

"A navvy," Blackstone said.

"Just a navvy? – Not many navvies try and get cocky with me. Those that do usually end up with their throats cut."

Blackstone said: "Then you should employ better bodyguards." He took some snuff. "That cove they call the Gorger. Rely on him and you'll be a corpse tomorrow."

The king of the navvies considered this. After a while he said: "Talk like that, my dear, and you might be a corpse within five minutes." He puffed at his pipe. "Just what brings you here, Rookie?"

"You must know," Blackstone said. He held up his bandaged hands.

"Soft-belly hands, eh? So you've been inside I shouldn't wonder. On the run are you?" When Blackstone didn't reply Petro said: "I thought as much." He found another glass and poured them both gin. "I could peach on you, of course."

Blackstone said: "Petro, king of the navvies, peach on a navvy?" He shook his head. "You might do a lot of things, but you wouldn't do that."

Petro considered the compliment. "What you must accept," he said, after a couple of puffs on his belligerent little pipe, "is that there's only one person issuing orders round here. The owners might think they are, so might the contractors. But the only person who matters is me." He poured himself more gin. "If I wanted work to stop on the railway tomorrow it would stop – on my command."

"I don't doubt it," Blackstone said.

Petro said sharply: "What were you inside for?"

"Thieving," Blackstone said.

"What sort of thieving?"

"Rampsman," Blackstone said.

"Yes," said Petro in his rounded West Country voice, "I believe that. You've got the build." He leaned across and touched Blackstone's bandaged hands. "Don't take kindly to the shovels, do they. But I reckon other parts of you are tough enough after a few spells on the treadmill?"

"My legs are as tough as tree-trunks."

Petro roamed his palace. He wound the chiming clock and said: "You don't seem to be a drinking man, Rookie."

Blackstone swallowed his gin.

"That's better." Petro paced around. "I'll be honest with you, Rookie. I didn't like the sound of you when you arrived. You seemed to have an air about you." He swallowed the gin in one gulp. "I don't like coves with airs. Just the same, you've just put paid to one of my henchmen. And they don't fall easily because I pick 'em myself."

Blackstone waited.

Petro sat down at the table, pulled open a drawer and pulled out a pistol with an ornate butt. Spanish, Blackstone judged. Decrepit and unreliable. Petro played with the trigger in a way that made Blackstone suspect he was handier with a knife or a life-protector.

Petro said: "Don't get too sure of yourself."

"The man you sent to get me was a fat pig."

"Oh." Petro pulled at his ear-ring. "And you think you could beat up the rest of my bodyguards in the same way?"

"How many have you got?"

"Three," Petro said, "now you've eliminated the Gorger."

"All at once," Blackstone said, hoping that Petro didn't take him up on it.

"I told you not to get too sure of yourself." He drummed strong fingers on the table. "The trouble is that you're a bit of a mystery. Suddenly arriving here with your fish-belly hands just as we're finishing the railway and half-killing one of my men." He gazed into his empty glass of gin. "I don't like mysteries around here."

"No mystery," Blackstone said.

"Perhaps not. You just seem different to the others. But there's one or two things navigators working for me have to understand. First of all, I have their welfare at heart. I am their leader, no one else. Whatever I do is for their benefit. I negotiate between the navvies and the contractors. I get them a fair deal. And I charge them 1d a month. That's about 300 pennies. Is that fair?"

"Very reasonable," Blackstone said. "And you want me to help you collect the contributions?"

Petro smiled with a flash of gold somewhere in the back of his mouth. "I may want you to replace the Gorger."

Blackstone said: "What do I get out of it?"

Petro squeezed the last drops out of the gin bottle into their glasses. "A little bit extra, culley. A little bit extra." He swallowed his gin. "In fact, there might be quite a bit more in it for you if you play your cards right. There are one or two things afoot...."

"Such as what?"

"Never you mind. Ask no questions and you'll get told no lies." The king of the navvies tapped his nose. "Be patient, Rookie. And don't cross me. Understand?"

"I understand."

"Good. And next time I summon you perhaps you'll come a little quicker."

"Perhaps," Blackstone said.

"I've got a feeling about you, Rookie."

"What sort of a feeling?"

"I don't know. We could get on famously. Or we could be the death of each other."

"Is that everything?" Blackstone asked.

"Aye, Rookie, that's everything."

Outside the bull terrier was still gnarling and the mongrel's lip was lifted as if it had got stuck on its sharp white teeth.

The missionary was waiting for him near The Rectory. She had distributed her tracts to the men sitting around the fires while protected by Petro's bodyguard, a big-bearded man with a Cornish wrestler's girth.

"Mr Rookie," she said, "you've got to help me."

"In what way, ma'am?"

"He'll listen to you."

"Who, Petro?"

She nodded eagerly, the Bible under her arm. There was a smell of cooking on the air and some of the navvies were singing:

We are the navigators,
Dressed as sharp as alligators,
When we go out on the randy,
Down the Strand with a bottle of brandy,

We dress sharper still like a crockodilly,
Just in case we reach Piccadilly.

Blackstone saw a falling star. It was a deep, innocent night and the girl was part of it.

He said: "I'm sorry, there's nothing I can do."

"He'll listen to you," she repeated. "He likes you, I know it."

"With respect, ma'am, you're not much judge of human relationships."

She looked around as if someone might be listening and said: "You don't speak like a navvy, Mr Rookie. In fact with that waistcoat you look quite a beau."

"Most navvies have got waistcoats like this," he said. "Perhaps it's my London accent."

"Perhaps." She peered at him so closely that a girl lying in the embrace of a navvy and sharing a bottle with him shouted: "Do you fancy him, luv?"

Josephine Courtney stepped back. "I'm sorry," she said to Blackstone.

"No need to be."

"It's just that I'm sure I've seen you somewhere before."

"I haven't seen you, ma'am."

"Ah well, I must be mistaken." Her face was very earnest in the jumping firelight. "But you will try and help me, won't you? If Mr Petro tells them to come to my services then they'll come." She hesitated. "And you, Mr Rookie, you'll come?"

"If you don't mind a congregation of one."

"There'll be more," she said with finality. "If you have a word with Mr Petro...."

The bodyguard said: "Come along, miss. For your own good. It's a good mile from here and Petro said to get you home by ten sharp."

After she had gone Blackstone glanced at the sermon in the tract. It wasn't optimistic. "If you should be killed by a fall of rock, if you should fall victim to smallpox, if you should catch a disease from foul meat sold at the tommy shops, ask yourself: Am I ready to enter the Kingdom of God?"

Blackstone, who didn't think he was quite ready, handed the tract to the girl in the navvy's arms and went to his bunk.

Chapter Four

Blackstone hunted for Frying Pan Charlie – the informer, the nose – for a week. But he was elusive, as if he knew someone was looking for him.

Blackstone went first to his residence, a long burrow in a grassy bank shored-up and roofed with planks. It housed twenty men and four women – two of them wives – on straw mattresses laid side by side.

Its crone told Blackstone that Frying Pan Charlie had left a week ago; but he hadn't gone far because he had left his belongings.

The crone protested when Blackstone started to go through his belongings. Blackstone gave her a shilling. He found: a rainbow waistcoat. A hammer. A torn shirt. A crust of bread as hard as charity. A letter from his mother, probably written by a screever, asking for money because "things were desperate". A mould for making bullets.

Blackstone thanked the crone but she didn't reply; just went on humming a lullaby to a baby she had nursed aeons ago.

He questioned the railway gang with which Frying Pan had worked; but questions were as welcome as the pox among navvies. Frying Pan's workmate was easier because he had a grudge. "Find the bastard," he said, "and bring him back here."

"Any idea where he's gone?"

The navvy's name was Claret because his nose bled easily when he fought; he worked for the Golden Horn gang who frequented a tavern of that name. He leaned on his shovel. "Could be anywhere," he said, "the bloody Irish mick."

Blackstone said: "Unusual, isn't it – a mick working along the line? They usually keep the Scots at one end and the Irish at the other."

Claret said: "He'd work anywhere, the bastard." He kicked some earth from his shovel. "He's not like the rest of the Irish. They've got some pride." He examined the blade. "Frying Pan would wriggle in anywhere he thought the going was easy."

"And it's easy here?"

"By comparison." Claret wiped the sweat from his forehead. "But I wish to God Frying Pan was back here with me to help shift this lot."

"How hard is it?" Blackstone asked.

"It's like this," Claret said. "We're each supposed to lift twenty tons of muck a day and load it on to the wagons." He pointed at the horse-drawn trains which took the earth and rocks along the embankments. "But the work's almost finished here. Frying Pan could sense when the working was becoming easy and he could sense when it was coming to an end. That's why he left, I suppose, because the railway's nearly finished. You see," he explained, "two of us work as a team. Between the two of us we fill fourteen wagons – seven each. We've got a sort of rhythm going. When one's gone the other can't fill five, let alone seven …" He stared suspiciously at Blackstone. "But you must know that."

"I know it," Blackstone said, feeling the scabs on his hands. "Where do you think he's gone?"

"Where the going's easy," Claret said. "Somewhere behind where they're cleaning up. Mind you" – he spat on his hands – "the money won't be so good but I expect Frying Pan's found a way of making it up. He usually does."

Blackstone looked towards Darlington, towards Witton Park Colliery, the western limit of the railroad. "So he's back there somewhere."

"I suppose so. Why are you so interested?"

Blackstone shrugged. "A debt to pay."

"Ah," said Claret, as if that explained everything. "He does owe a lot of brass, does Frying Pan. In fact he owes me a bender." He warmed to Blackstone. "Good luck, culley. If you find him bring him back here."

During his search for Frying Pan Charlie, so named because he always cooked in a black pan deep with grease, Blackstone visited the tommy shop.

It was owned by the contractor, Edward Pascoe, and it was guarded by dogs. Pascoe sold bad meat – tommy rot – and watered ale. The navvies were paid once a month and for most of the time lived on credit. In exchange for tokens Pascoe handed over his rotting food, short-weight at high prices.

Pascoe was a furtive man with larded hair and a small red nose buttoned on his face. "Why should I know where Frying Pan Charlie is?" he asked.

"You know him then?"

Blackstone examined the sides of meat, furred with green, slabs of rancid butter and barrels of diluted ale. The dogs eyed him from the doorway of the wooden hut.

Pascoe laughed. "Frying Pan Charlie? There are a dozen Frying Pans on this stretch of the track. Which one do you want?"

Blackstone described him. An Irishman. Small and sprightly, loquacious but evasive, inclined to talk too much when he'd had a few wets.

Pascoe was amused. "You've described at least a dozen of my customers," he said. "So I can't help you."

"Who do you work for?"

"For myself."

"No one else?"

"I'm a contractor in my own right."

"So you issue the tokens and then collect them again in exchange for your own goods?"

Pascoe shrugged.

"I should have thought you would have remembered a man like Frying Pan Charlie. He must have been after credit."

"They're all after credit, my dear. My whole business is founded on credit." He smiled. "Are you after credit, Rookie?"

"Not your sort of credit, Pascoe." He took his Nathaniel Mills snuffbox from his pocket. "Do you operate as a pawn-shop as well?"

Pascoe looked at the snuffbox greedily. "Why, do you want to pawn anything?"

"Do navvies pawn their possessions with you?"

"Occasionally. Had you anything in mind?" Sunlight lay warmly on the smooth gold snuffbox.

Blackstone shook his head. "Not at the moment. But I had thought about giving you a price for that – when you're free to sell it." He pointed at the black frying pan, recently polished, hanging on the wall like a pendulum.

Pay-day and no pay.

The navvies who had been planning to go on the randy gathered in the field waiting for Petro's lead. The day's heat was veiled in the morning sky; butterflies flirted over the embankment and there was a smell of frying bacon in the air.

Blackstone sat outside The Rectory with his dog, watching trouble assemble. He knew why there was no pay – because the money was being delivered two days late – and vaguely felt he should prevent it. But his baton was twenty miles away at The Naked Man, his assignment was highway robbery and he was developing an affinity with the navvies. His shoulder muscles ached and his hands were still raw; but yesterday he had filled six wagons.

But the day had been marred by a death. A young Welshman planning to emigrate to America had been engulfed by a fall of earth. The navvies organized a fund, gave his widow £5 and planned an ambitious funeral. They were used to funerals, they were part of the routine.

Yankee Tom sat beside Blackstone chewing tobacco. He said: "It's going to be a hell of a day." He stretched and spat. He was lean and easy and his life was a secret.

Blackstone asked: "What brought you to England, Yankee?"

"A boat," Yankee Tom said. He stuck another wad of tar-black tobacco in his mouth and sank his teeth into it with pleasure.

"Are you going back?"

"Maybe. Maybe not. What brought you here?"

"My feet," Blackstone said.

"You've never been a navvy. What's more you've never been in jail. I can tell," he added, losing some of his secrecy. "You haven't got the colour of a man who's been in jail."

"How would you know?"

"Doesn't matter how I'd know. I just know, that's all."

He didn't ask any more questions and friendship was established on what they didn't know about each other.

At the other end of the field, Josephine Courtney climbed on to a tea-chest. She held up her hands, ignoring the ribald remarks. "I have a message for you," she shouted. She possessed a good, carrying voice for so slight a physique.

"We don't want messages, we want our brass," a navvy shouted.

She held up her hands again. "I know what you men have been through. I ask you to have patience..."

"To hell with patience, lady."

"... in the name of God."

God quietened them a little. Josephine Courtney seized her opportunity. "I know what you men are planning and I know how you feel. I, too, have been without money. But anger isn't the answer and rioting will only bring retribution. I implore you to have patience. God is looking after you...."

It was too much for one of them. "Where was he when Taffy was killed yesterday?"

Miss Courtney smiled patiently. "Taffy is in a better place now. Taffy is in heaven."

"Taffy wanted to go to America."

"There really is no comparison," Josephine Courtney said. She looked benignly at her flock of hairy-chested communicants. "What I want you to do is pray. Obviously there has been a misunderstanding over your pay. The harder you pray the sooner your money will come. Have faith. Settle down in your homes and spend the day with your wives." She looked doubtfully at the tallywomen at the back of the congregation. "Blessed are the peacemakers for they are the children of God."

Yankee Tom said: "She got that wrong.... for they *shall be called* the children of God."

"What were you," Blackstone said, "a prison chaplain?"

"What were you," Yankee Tom asked, "a parish constable?"

The veil had lifted from the sky and it was deep and blue and hot. Dogs sought the shade, babies cried and the men sweated in their best clothes which they always wore for a riot. Liquor was the remedy for most ills so they drank ale to cool themselves and sweated all the more.

Josephine Courtney stamped her foot on the tea-chest, making it wobble. "I know you men are planning to ... to go on the randy as you call it. To go on the spree. Perhaps this hold-up is a blessing in disguise." She held her arms wide to quell the passions blossoming this sweltering day. "I know what you're thinking. You want your pleasures." She didn't enumerate them. "Why not spend a day of contemplation to prepare yourself for tomorrow, Sunday." She tossed them her final inducement. "Tomorrow I shall be holding a service here at eleven in the morning."

Petro's yellow door opened and the king of the navvies emerged, yellow Bristol colours around his neck, sealskin cap on the back of his head, ear-ring capturing the sunlight. He made his way to a cluster of beer barrels at the opposite end of the field from the missionary. Two bodyguards walked behind him with his bull terrier.

He mounted a barrel and addressed his subjects.

"So make today a day of peace," Josephine Courtney shouted.

"Today," Petro shouted, "we march."

The navvies roared their approval and Josephine Courtney climbed down from her tea-chest.

At least, Blackstone thought, she was receiving a lesson in oratory.

Cajoling, hectoring, threatening, Petro had them on his side within seconds. Although he *was* preaching to the converted.

He slammed a fist into the palm of the other hand. "I ask you – are we going to stand for this?"

"No, no, no," they answered him, fists clenched, eyes wild, intoxicated by words, by injustice, by the smell of violence which was part of this breathless day.

Petro held up his hands and they were instantly quiet. "This is the second time, lads. The first time they said the stagecoach had been robbed. But who robbed it, I wonder. Could it be them who want to keep you without money? Them who want to go on paying you with worthless tokens, forcing you to buy tommy rot, watered ale and gin?"

It could, the navvies shouted.

Yankee Tom said: "Better get your gun."

"How did you know I'd got one?" Blackstone kept the rusty pistol under his straw mattress.

"Alice told me." Yankee Tom stood up, tall and leathery, looking as if he needed a horse. "I'll get myself a cudgel."

Sweat gleamed on Petro's face. "Very well, men, we were asked to believe in the first robbery. And we did get paid – eventually. But there's been no robbery this time. No mysterious masked highwayman in the moonlight. I saw the stagecoach arrive safely in Stockton. No excuses this time. So where's the money? Where's the blunt?" He took a sheet of paper from his pocket and read it aloud. "We are sorry but there's been a delay. You will be paid on Monday." Petro stuck his thumbs in his belt. "They couldn't even face us, lads. A message delivered at night. Could anything be more cowardly?"

It couldn't, they shouted.

"I say let's show them that we won't stand for this treatment. Show them we're men, human-beings, not cattle waiting to be fed. Who the hell do they think they are?" He pitched his voice lower. "But I'll tell you what, today we'll show them who we are." His voice rose an octave. "Arm yourself, lads. It's the day of the navigators. Our hour has come."

The navvies dispersed to their huts; the dogs barked with excitement.

What should a Bow Street Runner do? Warn the magistrates, the local constables, the military? No time, Rookie decided.

Petro's army took up position behind him. About two hundred of them. The dogs behind. The women retired to prepare themselves for the army's return, boiling water to bathe broken heads with.

Blackstone left his gun behind. It offended him and he thought it might blow up. He stuck one of Alice's knives in his belt and helped himself to a cudgel.

Petro spotted him. "I want you here, Rookie, with my other lads." He turned to his troops. "Now remember, no damage to life or limb." He laughed and they laughed with him. He stepped out swinging one of his Indian clubs.

We are the navigators,
Dressed as sharp as alligators.

Tin whistles and drums took up the song. An army on the march. Blackstone was glad Birnie couldn't see its latest conscript.

Two miles along the railway Pascoe checked his stores. The smell of the meat was unpleasant and he held a handkerchief drenched with lavender water to his nose. He tested the new weights for his scales to make sure they were loaded in his favour. They were – far too light – and he grunted with satisfaction. He hurled a weight at a rat and altered the prices on bread, cheese and potatoes; he didn't lower them, he had never done that.

According to his information the pay-out of wages at the Masons' Arms tavern had been delayed until Monday; this meant that, over the weekend, the navvies would be spending tokens again – living on truck, on credit. With luck some of them would be so much in his debt that when they were paid they would be broke again. They only had themselves to blame, Pascoe decided.

He fingered his nose, a nervous habit he had acquired since the night he had gone to sleep after a week on the gin and awoken next morning with a cherry instead of a nose. He shovelled dirt and stones into the sacks of potatoes and went outside to water the beer.

There were two dozen barrels of it. Pascoe knew of contractors who made more money selling ale to navvies than from construction work. It was a difficult decision to make. Water the beer and make a profit or sell a strong brew which kept the navvies drunk and thirsting for more. There were two schools of thought and Pascoe hadn't made up his mind. His hero was a contractor said to have made £7,000 from tommy shops during the building of one canal. Pascoe had his own scheme for making capital on the S and D. But for the moment he was happy watering beer. He worked with such concentration that he didn't hear the distant sound of pipe and drum.

The vanguard of Petro's army reached him as he was sampling a pot of ale – before diluting it.

At first he wasn't frightened. Everyone knew he watered the ale: he wasn't caught in any act. He smiled. "What can I do for you gentlemen?" His larded hair gleamed as if it were melting.

"Nothing," Petro said. "There's nothing you can do." All the navvies were lined up behind him.

Pascoe's expression changed. "What do you want. What are you looking at me like that for?"

Blackstone tried unsuccessfully to feel sorry for him. He began to wish he'd brought the gun. What could he do if they tried to kill the contractor? A Bow Street Runner couldn't be an accessory to murder.

Petro said: "We want what's ours."

Pascoe began to tremble. "I don't understand."

"You will. Where do you keep the tokens we've paid you this month. In there?" He pointed at the shack standing beside the track.

"No," Pascoe said. His fingers found his nose and pulled at it; it looked loose, Blackstone thought.

"First we'll have some ale," Petro said.

Pascoe knelt and poured him a pot. Petro kicked it from his hands; then pushed him with his foot, sending him sprawling.

Pascoe said: "Don't you want any ale?"

"Not watered ale."

"That wasn't watered. Not that barrel." He sat up. "I was drinking it. That proves it wasn't watered, doesn't it?"

Petro gazed at him thoughtfully. "Like a drop of ale, do you?"

"In moderation."

Petro turned to Blackstone and the three henchmen. "Tie the greasy little bastard up."

They tied him to a barrel. Blackstone was becoming disgusted with it.

"That's right," Petro said. "That's fine. Now, what about a drop of watered ale, Pascoe? Sample some of the bog-water you've been selling to my men?" He picked up a funnel and shoved it into Pascoe's mouth. Then he filled a pot with ale from a watered barrel and poured it into the funnel. Pascoe swallowed desperately. Most of the beer went down his gullet, some of it down his windpipe. The level of the beer in the funnel sank, disappeared. Pascoe was retching and coughing.

"Right," Blackstone said, taking the funnel out of his mouth, "that'll teach him a lesson."

Petro said: "Who asked you to take it out?"

"You'll kill him if you keep doing that."

"So?" Petro patted the ornate butt of the Spanish pistol in his belt. "Not getting queasy, are you, Rookie?"

Blackstone decided that one more pot of ale wouldn't kill Pascoe.

Petro said: "Put the funnel back."

Blackstone replaced it, pretending to shove it hard down Pascoe's throat. "Hold it with your teeth," he whispered.

Petro filled another pot of ale and poured it down the funnel. Pascoe swallowed hard, but the beer poured through his nostrils. His face was scarlet and he made an ugly noise in the back of his throat.

The navvies watched uneasily.

Blackstone said: "Don't kill him, Petro. We're thirsty – don't waste the beer."

Petro knew when he was beaten, a rare quality of leadership. He also knew how to adapt defeat. He took the pistol from his belt, cocked it and fired into the sky. "Pascoe won't cheat us again, lads. Now get stuck into the beer. Each to his own."

They cheered him and charged the barrels.

They found pots, buckets, saucepans. They used their caps, cupped hands. They hacked rents in the sides of the barrels and lay on the grass with the beer gushing into their mouths. For two hours they drank until the air around them was fermented.

Midday. The sun splintered with heat.

"Now the lightning," Petro shouted. "And the rum and whisky." He went into the shack and handed out the bottles. They drank the spirits as though they were still drinking ale.

Petro brought a sack of tickets. "Your tokens, lads," he said. He lit them and they watched their debts burn.

"Good old Petro."

"Petro for ever."

Petro walked over to Blackstone. "Still sober, culley? Here, have a drink." He handed him a bottle of gin. "That's better," he observed as Blackstone drank. "We don't want anyone sober around here. Wouldn't be right, would it, Rookie?" He slapped his stomach. "Now we'll help ourselves to a little tommy. Even if it is rotten."

He gave the order and the men brought out cheeses, loaves, sides of bacon, sacks of potatoes. They piled it on the railway, some of them falling with their loads.

"And now," Petro said, "a bonfire." He splashed spirits on the walls of the shack.

Accessory to arson, Blackstone thought.

"Marvellous what the heat of the sun will do, isn't it?" He made a torch from some rum-soaked rags wrapped round a cudgel, lit it and tossed it on to the roof of the tommy shop.

Small flames, almost invisible, covered the shack with a bluish, incandescent cloak. The wood caught and the cloak turned orange. Smoke and sparks poured into the sky; the rats made a run for it. While the dogs chased them the men finished the liquor. Then the sport was over.

"What now, Petro?" someone called.

"What now?" Petro tightened his yellow handkerchief and fanned himself with his sealskin cap. "What now? I think it's time we went on the randy, lads. We mightn't have got any brass but we've had enough booze to float the hulks to Van Diemen's Land. What say we go to the village?"

"To the village," they bawled.

Pipe and drum started up, rhythm confused.

They took up marching order. Petro, bodyguards, troops, dogs. By now, Blackstone thought, magistrates and constables would be alerted. And possibly the Dragoons. Local newspaper editors would be clearing a column for the account of the riot. If they knew a Bow Street Runner was marching with the navvies they would clear a page. Head erect, cudgel in hand, he marched towards the dock, the cell, the gallows.

Word had reached the village. Doors were bolted, windows shuttered. The village was a single street with a church at one end rebuking revelry and a tavern at the other defying rectitude. In between were the cottages. It was hot and deserted. No one had warned the bellringers and the notes hung, lozenges of sound, on the sleepy air.

They stopped outside the tavern, where two of Petro's henchmen broke down the doors. They didn't wait for a command: they had done it before. An advance guard took the tavern, handing out spoils to the reinforcements. The bells pealed melodiously in rehearsal for Sunday.

Blackstone joined Petro in the tavern. "Enjoying yourself, culley?" Petro asked, blue eyes bright in his brown face.

Blackstone nodded.

"You don't look too happy." He squeezed Blackstone's arm. "Relax. No one can touch us – there's no military for fifty miles around." He lit his stubby pipe. "Stick with me, Rookie, and you'll find a lot of good things coming your way. There's something brewing I haven't told you about."

Petro had to boast, Blackstone thought; which meant that, as a criminal, he was an amateur. But the highway robbery hadn't been amateurish. It was an intriguing thought.

Petro surveyed his troops spilling out of the tavern into the sunlight. "One thing's missing, Rookie – women. We need some molls. Are you fond of molls?"

Gratefully, Blackstone reverted to the truth. He said he was.

Petro said: "My bitch left me. The bitch," he added in his repetitive way. Then, suspecting that he had revealed weakness, he said: "I gave her a good hiding. That's why she left. Good riddance. Good riddance I say."

Blackstone waited.

"So we'll get ourselves some molls," Petro said. "That's what we'll do. Come with me, Rookie. And you," he said, grabbing a bodyguard.

They walked down the hot wide street.

Petro stopped outside a blue-painted door and rapped the brass knocker. "The town crier," he told them. "The village crier if you like." He knocked again but there was no reply. Petro fired his pistol. "Come on out," he shouted, "or we'll knock the door down."

A movement inside. The door inched open. A man's face, a voice faltering with fear. Petro pushed the door and the man fell back, a plump countryman with a whiskered face and a bald head. "What do you want?"

"Your services," Petro said. "Have you got your bell?"

The man nodded at the brass hand-bell on the hallstand. "Bring it with you," Petro said.

The church bells were fading. A few notes lingered until the crier pushed them aside with his bell. "Bring out your women," he cried. "Bring out your women."

The villagers acted craftily. They pushed into the street all the women who had previously accommodated navvies on the randy. There were eight of them, a good turn-out for a small community. Petro had one on his arm, so did Blackstone; the other six were fraternizing with the drunken navvies in the churchyard.

Blackstone slipped his arm round the waist of his girl.

"What's your name?" she asked.

"Rookie."

"That's a funny name." She had a broad Lancashire accent.

"I'm a funny fellow."

"I think you're nice. Different somehow. How about a kiss."

Blackstone looked out of the tavern doorway and exclaimed.

"What's the matter?"

Down the street he had seen the determined figure of Josephine Courtney.

'I'll be back in a minute," he said.

"Well, really," she said.

Petro said: "Where are you going?" He had eased one of his girl's breasts out of her dress and was squeezing it.

"A sermon's on its way," Blackstone said.

"You fix her, Rookie. You fix it." He found a partner for the breast.

"You," Josephine Courtney said. "I wouldn't have thought it of you."

"Why not, ma'am?"

She didn't reply. "I'm going to get a magistrate to read the Riot Act."

"I shouldn't if I were you. They'll kill him."

"Where are the rest of the men?"

Blackstone pointed to the churchyard where there was a good deal of movement and noise.

"What are they doing?"

"They're not praying."

"It's disgusting," she said. But there was more than disgust in her voice; a blade of hatred which he hadn't heard before.

"I agree with you."

"Then what are you doing here?"

Blackstone wished he could tell her. He tried to explain about the wages, about exploitation, about injustice. He spoke gently. "There's nothing we can do." He tried to explain that, so far, not much harm had been done. But she didn't understand.

"You look strong," she told him. "But you're weak."

He took her arm. "I suggest you leave as quietly as possible," he said, calculating that six women to a couple of hundred drunken navvies was a poor equation. "Otherwise you might come to harm."

She frowned. "Let me look at you." She stepped back. "Now walk a few steps."

"Walk, ma'am?"

"Yes," she said firmly, "walk."

He took half a dozen steps. "I've got it," she said. "The highwayman."

"I beg your pardon?"

"It was the highwayman you reminded me of. You see, I was in the coach when he took the wages. You've got the same build, the same air about you. But he had a limp."

She shook her head with finality. "No, we haven't met before."

The significance of what she had said only came to him much later because at that moment the fighting started.

The churchyard brawl – or riot as it was later described – had commonplace beginnings. It was over women: there weren't enough to go round and one of the navvies jumped the queue.

It developed quickly with old scores being settled. Old soldier fought old sailor; Lancashire versus Yorkshire; Cornish wrestler versus prizefighter; railroad bookie versus debtor.

The girls fought, too, clawing and gouging, grateful that they weren't damaging their clothes because they had already taken them off.

After a while the villagers, noting laborious punches and slurred reflexes, emerged from their cottages, and joined in. They fought the navvies who had taken their girls and drunk their liquor: they fought the railway that was going to take their living.

Cudgels swung and the men fell unconscious on the graves above the freshly-buried and the ancient dead.

The missionary said: "What are you going to do?"

"There's nothing I can do. It won't last long. They're all too moppy. Drunk," he explained.

He looked round for Petro but the king of the navvies had retired upstairs with his girl.

A navvy named Pigtail Clancy came up to them and stroked Josephine Courtney's face. "You'll do," he said.

"Take your hands off," Blackstone said.

Pigtail's hand dropped to her breast and Blackstone hit him in the belly with his left fist, clipped him on the chin with his right. Then he pulled him by his pigtail to the side of the road.

"Thank you," she said, as if she were accepting silver for the morning collection.

Behind a gravestone someone discharged a pistol, sending the crows flying from the chestnut trees. Then another shot. The fighting slowed down, stopped. The villagers who wanted no part in a shooting match retired.

It took half an hour to clear the churchyard. The navvies helped each other and limped away towards Shanty Town, heads bleeding, knuckles grazed, an army in retreat.

Doors and shutters opened and life returned as if someone had inserted a key and wound the village up.

One figure didn't move. It lay between two gravestones under a chestnut tree.

Blackstone turned the man over. He had been shot in the chest and, looking at his dead, staring features, Blackstone knew instinctively that his search for Frying Pan Charlie was over.

Chapter Five

Sir Richard Birnie read the newspaper with annoyance.
"A disgusting affray in which the behaviour of the navvies sank to unplumbed depths of degradation. We had a mind to liken their acts of drunken brutality to the behaviour of animals; but that would be a slur on the noble horse, the faithful canine friend." The newspaper made no mention of the villagers' contribution to the brawl. "These savages, having plundered a humble tavern, proceeded to desecrate Holy ground by belabouring each other with fists and cudgels in the adjoining churchyard. Surely the gallows is the only punishment to fit such blasphemous crimes. One man, apparently known as Frying Pan Charlie, died during this loathsome exhibition of physical violence and, in our view, this makes all the navvies accessories. However," said the leader-writer magnanimously, "we are prepared to acknowledge that the men were in liquor and not wholly responsible for their deplorable actions. Transportation to some far-flung corner of the globe would, perhaps, be the most desirable solution, serving the dual purposes of providing undeveloped countries with a labour force whose rowdyism would soon be dissipated in the great wide-open spaces and ridding this country of a pestilence. Let it be hoped," the writer added, "that those who misguidedly support the construction of

railways realize, before it is too late, what mischief they are fermenting on this green land of ours."

No mention of the canal navvies' mischief, Birnie noted. He climbed out of the four-poster bed and began to shave with the boiling water brought by a maid. It was 9am and in an hour he was taking part in an archery practice with his host, Sir Geoffrey Hawkins, toxophilite, eccentric and sworn enemy of the railways.

He shaved carefully, aware that his anger might draw blood. He was angry for several reasons, all of them connected with Blackstone.

Blackstone had failed to send a report to him. Presumably because he had nothing to report.

But there had been action. Oh yes, Birnie thought, bitterly, there had been action. There had been a riot!

According to the newspaper, all the navvies from Shanty Town had been there. Presumably that included Blackstone. A Bow Street Runner in a riot. If Peel ever found out! Birnie cut the flesh just below his nose.

He stemmed the blood with the towel. It stopped quite soon. Old blood. He shaved on.

Originally there had been one lead, the informant called Frying Pan Charlie. Now deceased. Murdered, it seemed, in Blackstone's presence. Birnie cut himself just below the ear.

He had often questioned his wisdom in promoting Blackstone to his élite plain-clothes police force admired throughout the world. A Runner from the Rookery, the underworld, the other side of the law. Birnie had wondered which side held Blackstone's deepest loyalties. But gradually his doubts had receded as Blackstone proved himself to be the best thief-catcher in the team.

Now the doubts had returned. The women, the drinking, the mysterious informants who surfaced from

Blackstone's past and led him to his quarry. How many deals had Blackstone done? Interviewing the victim of a robbery, finding the thief and reaching a compromise. Eighty per cent of the swag returned to the victim; ten per cent for the thief, ten per cent for the Runner.

Birnie cut himself a third time. But what have we achieved? he asked the gritty old face staring at him from the mirror. He was in the enemy camp and he had learned nothing.

He dried his face and began to dress in his black clothes. He felt confused as he often did when he was involved with Blackstone. Shaking his head, he walked down the broad staircase to the baronial hall where the enemy awaited him with a bow and arrow in his hand.

Birnie approached Sir Geoffrey Hawkins warily. He had met many eccentrics in London society and knew that eccentricity was a rich man's luxury: if you were poor you were mad.

Sir Geoffrey was a duellist of renown, a hard rider to hounds, a man's man, a bully. He beat his servants and paid them handsomely. His current obsession was the despoiling of the countryside by trains: his eccentricity was little girls which he bought in London's Windmill Street.

He had returned to his mansion, where Birnie had been staying the night before, and archery was the order of the day. Archery took Birnie back to his youth, back to Banff in Scotland, before he had journeyed to London with his ambition; long before the Prince of Wales had asked for "that young Scots saddlemaker" in Macintosh's in the Haymarket; centuries before he had been made a magistrate and knighted and had begun to suspect that he may have been betrayed by his ambition. The moors and the heather and mountains in the distance pulling showers out of the clouds. A bow in his hand and a butt quivering with arrows. Birnie wondered if his old arms had kept any of their skills over the years; if his eyes could still pick out the gold. At least he knew enough about archery to deflate Hawkins a little; Birnie enjoyed small pleasures.

Hawkins shook his hand with a fierce grip. He was a huge man, handsome features marred by a nose broken at the Pugilistic Club. His eyes were blue, his brow noble, and it was difficult to decide which particular feature betrayed his madness. The eyebrows perhaps; they should have been thick and virile and they were as thin as a boy's moustache.

"I trust you've breakfasted well," Sir Geoffrey said.

"Sufficiently," said Birnie, who had discarded the liver, kidneys and beefsteak and eaten only the porridge and toast.

"Have you any experience with arrows?"

"A little."

"Let's go on the lawn then." They walked across the flagstones to the studded doors. A footman opened them. Summer greeted them, breathless, latent, gathering its powers. But, despite the drought, the lawns of the Hawkins mansion – turreted and incongruous as if it had been transported from the Black Forest – were salad green.

A footman handed Birnie bow, quiver and arrows. He felt like an elderly Robin Hood.

Hawkins, in his squire's tweeds despite the heat, said: "I have a feeling, Birnie, that the reason for your visit isn't entirely social."

Birnie squinted at the butt one hundred yards away. Perhaps they could start at sixty yards? He snapped: "I'm here because you invited me."

"You're here," Hawkins said, "because you're interested in this bloody railway." He pulled the silk string experimentally. "As you know, I detest everything it stands for, but we mustn't let that spoil our friendship. What bothers me," he added, "is whether your visit is professional."

"How could it be?" They were standing beside an ornamental fountain and its cool sound made Birnie feel hot in his black clothes.

Hawkins put down his bow. "I'm not sure. There's a lot of money behind steam locomotion. A lot of power. We've got the Liverpool–Manchester Bill chucked out – thanks to that ignorant buffoon Stephenson." Hawkins looked at him shrewdly from beneath his pale eyebrows. "But that's only one round in the battle. Could it be that Bow Street has been called in to investigate the legality of the situation?"

Birnie said: "You sound like a constable giving evidence. What the devil are you talking about?"

"You know – riots, posters. Perhaps Eccleston or someone has suggested that we're inciting trouble." He looked inquiringly at Birnie.

Birnie was relieved. He said: "The visit is purely social. But I can't deny I'm enjoying the proximity to the railway." He shaded his eyes and gazed across the lawns, across the estate, towards the line. "I've had a good look at it. In a few days' time I shall be going to Newcastle. To see Stephenson," he added slyly. "Then I'll go back to London. But I should like to attend the opening of the railroad."

"If it's ever opened," Hawkins said. "It wouldn't surprise me if Stephenson's engine didn't blow up first."

"You've been reading your own pamphlets," Birnie said. "Danger of exploding boilers killing passengers? Cinders setting fire to hay-stacks? The end of the farm worker?" He looked longingly at the bubbling water. "Really, Hawkins, you do let your imagination run away with you. Perhaps there *is* a case for incitement to riot."

"I'm not the only one who thinks like that."

"No," Birnie agreed. "There's Lord Derby and Lord Sefton and all the canal owners and every short-sighted reactionary landowner in the land."

"There's more disagreement than that." Hawkins picked up his bow and caressed the ash with thick fingers. "What about the Stockton versus Darlington affair? Stockton wanted to build the line without touching Darlington. Then there's the row between the locomotive men and the drivers of the horse-drawn trains. Did you know they were going to have both on the S and D?"

Birnie, who thought he knew everything there was to know about the railway, nodded. Loops had been built to allow the horse-drawn trains to get out of the way of the locomotives; but the drivers were threatening to ignore them and block the steam engines.

"And the navvies, of course," Hawkins said.

"What about the navvies?"

"They could wreck anything. Particularly with Scots and Irish involved. Did you read that article about the riot near Shanty Town?"

"An appalling piece of journalism."

"I rather enjoyed it," Hawkins said. "After all, I wrote it." He looked at his watch. "How about it? Six arrows each. Canals versus railways. Horse versus steam."

"Backwardness versus progress," Birnie said, flexing his right arm and feeling a puny response from his thin bicep.

"I'll give you an extra arrow for a practice shot," Hawkins said. "I've been getting my hand in at night. It's the only way, you know. Shooting at a lamp. Stops you from looking at your hand instead of the target."

"We'll have six each," Birnie said, wishing Hawkins would suggest sixty yards, eighty even.

"Just as you like. Don't forget I was in the Artillery Company. We've got quite a tradition, you know. I'll lend you some books while you're here. *The Bowman's Glory* by Sir William Wood. A first edition. When they buried the old boy at St James in Clerken well they shot three flights of whistling arrows across his grave."

Hawkins took a gold sovereign from his pocket and told Birnie to call. Birnie called wrongly.

"You shoot first." Hawkins despatched a footman to the butt. "I sometimes have a little sport with the servants," he told Birnie. "Just to keep my eye in. I make them run between those two trees." He pointed at two elm trees. "Then I fire a few arrows at them. Keeps them nippy."

He was, Birnie reflected, quite cracked.

Warily the footman took up a position ten yards from the butt.

"Off you go," said Sir Geoffrey. "Stand nice and up-right."

Birnie was standing as upright as he ever did.

"Left foot forward. Right hand drawn back to right pap as they used to say. Nearer your ear these days. A nice smart discharge. Allow for the side wind."

The target was four feet in diameter. It looked the size of a button. Birnie closed one eye: white, blue, red and gold fused into one indefinite colour. He thought he might kill the footman.

The arrow failed to reach the butt.

Hawkins was sympathetic. "Not quite strong enough. You should be smarter with your discharge."

Birnie's youth – the moors and the heather – receded. He selected another arrow, tipped with the wing feathers of a grey goose, and let fly.

"One scored," shouted the footman as the arrow hit the outer white circle.

"Better," said Hawkins. Horse was beating steam; old against new. "But not good enough." He laughed richly. "Remember what's at stake."

Birnie fired his remaining arrows. Two more whites, a blue and one red – just. No golds. Thirteen scored.

"Unlucky for some," Hawkins remarked jubilantly. He shouted to the footman: "Get nearer to the butt. Keeps them on their toes," he explained to Birnie.

"You must pay them well."

"Bloody well."

His first arrow landed in the blue. He swore. The next two in the red, almost in the golden eye. "That's it, I'm afraid," he said. "I've already beaten your score." But when you followed the hounds, kept falcons and indulged in pugilism the sporting instinct was always strong. "Tell you what," he said. "One arrow. Nearest the gold wins. Are you game?"

"Why not? I've got nothing to lose."

"How about a little wager on the side. Say twenty-five guineas?"

"I'm not a betting man."

"Just as you please."

Perhaps it was the heat. Perhaps it was a lifetime of inhibitions and subordination to rules; the doubts this morning as to whether any of it had been worth it. How many times had he lectured prisoners about the evils of gambling? "Make it fifty guineas," he said.

"Are you sure?"

"Of course I'm sure." Birnie was glad Blackstone was far away.

"Just as you please. It seems a lot of money, though."

"I'm not a pauper." Birnie felt giddy and would have liked to dip his face in the fountain. A thrush sang cool notes behind them, making Birnie feel even hotter.

"You're a sport," Hawkins said admiringly. "I'll give you that. Toss for it?"

Birnie nodded, leaning on the wall around the fountain. He thought he might faint.

"Your call."

Birnie called and won. "You first," he said. He wondered what his wife would say about the fifty guineas.

Hawkins selected an arrow with care. Tested the flight and the shaft.

The arrow flew beautifully, straight and true just inside the golden eye.

Hawkins said: "The money will go towards printing more leaflets." He grinned. "With your help we might even get the Manchester–Liverpool bill thrown out a second time."

"Don't be too sure," Birnie said. He was astonished with himself. An old man making a fool of himself. "There's no fool like an old fool." How many times had he said that to old gentlemen who had been blackmailed by dollymops and their flashmen?

Wearily he chose an arrow and took up his stance. He may even have shut his eyes; he wasn't sure. When the arrow left the bow he felt as though he were releasing his life.

"Gold," shouted the footman.

Birnie walked to the butt with Hawkins. Dead centre of the gold eye.

Hawkins swore, then blasphemed, the sporting instinct elusive for the moment. "I'll make you out a cheque," he said.

"Very well," Birnie said. "It'll buy a few miles of railway, no doubt."

※ ※ ※

Blackstone's report delivered by the driver of a post-chaise was brief.

It said: "The investigation is progressing satisfactorily." Despite one riot and one murder, Birnie thought.

"But I need your help. Can you please obtain for me the mould Sir Geoffrey Hawkins uses for making his bullets."

Steal it, Birnie thought. That's what he means. He wants the chief Bow Street magistrate to become a thief!

He smiled to himself, feeling his features crack. Why not? Gambler, thief. By nightfall he would be chasing the dollymops down the corridors.

Chapter Six

Blackstone decided to take his problems to sleep with him, hoping that he might wake up with the answers.

He had started with one highway robbery. He had expected a second attempt either on the empty stagecoach or the one carrying the wages two days later – the delay that had caused the riot. Nothing.

Instead he had a murder.

Why had Frying Pan Charlie been killed? Presumably because he had nosed; because he knew too much.

But about what? He had reported a conspiracy to Stephenson. Such a conspiracy was possible and the chief suspect was Petro, possibly working with the other bodyguards.

But how did they *know* that Frying Pan had peached on them?

The more he puzzled the more sleep receded.

At first he hadn't paid much attention to the details of the robbery. Now he remembered the touches of professionalism. The accomplice drawing the fire, for instance.

Something was eluding him.

The snores were thick around him. Alice's rocking chair creaked with its incessant rhythm. A couple made love. An owl hooted.

Blackstone continued to worry. The robbery had been professional, the murder amateurish. If the killer wanted people to think Frying Pan had died in the riot he had been hopelessly optimistic because the body was cold when Blackstone found it. Yet the two crimes were linked.

The couple spent their passion and were quiet. The rocking chair creaked on. A navvy cried out in his sleep – "Run for it, the rock's falling."

Blackstone dozed.

When he awoke at 3am Josephine Courtney's words were whispering in his brain. "It was the highwayman you reminded me of.... But he had a limp."

And Blackstone realized just how professional the robbery had been.

In a room above a chandler's in Darlington the highwayman, Henry Challoner, more often an assassin, checked details of the impending train robbery for the fourth time. These were his most valued weapons: planning and timing. He was a meticulous man and that was how he had stayed alive.

He wasn't happy with the assignment. There were too many imponderables. The speed of the locomotive during its trials depended on the number of wagons it would be pulling. Challoner didn't know how many wagons there would be; nor did anyone else. There was no certainty about the time the train would reach the point where he planned to board it; it was quite possible the engine would blow up before it got there

But there were compensations. His fee! The knowledge that Blackstone was working against him.

Both men born in the Rookery. Under different roofs but so alike that there had to be a connection. A relationship? Challoner shied away from the word. But the Rookery was a confused and fertile place in which privacy was as exceptional as honesty.

Challoner poured himself a whisky and stared at himself in a mirror. For a moment Blackstone stared back in the flickering candle-light. Tough, calm features bearing a few seams of hardship. But there wasn't any compassion or humour in this face – Blackstone faded.

Challoner downed his whisky. He was jealous of the differences in Blackstone's features. They could have been his and he didn't understand why Blackstone had been allowed them. The compassion was complacency protected by the law; Blackstone was a traitor to their birthright.

He sat down at the table and stared at his maps and diagrams. He was becoming interested in the drawing of Stephenson's engine and this annoyed him because hobbies were luxuries denied to professional assassins.

But the odd locomotive with its absurd smokestack inspired some sort of emotion in him; surely not affection.

He studied the details. Ten-foot-long boiler made with lap-jointed plates. Flue eighteen inches in diameter running from end to end with a heating surface of fifty to fifty-two square feet. The fire on a grate about four square feet. The whole engine weighed between six and eight tons. The weight interested Challoner because it would affect speed; speed was vital and was difficult to determine because the Stephenson school was inclined to boast. Eight miles an hour, ten, fifteen. ... Challoner thought fifteen was too much. Back to the number of wagons. It had been stated that eight was the maximum. But according to his information Stephenson intended the locomotive to pull thirty-two wagons and a coach at the opening on 27 September. How many would he experiment with on the trials?

One factor alarmed Challoner. This was the braking power of the engine: it was non-existent. Once you shut off steam the engine stopped fairly quickly, but again that was determined by the number of wagons. The alternative was for the driver to dodge round the rear moving eccentric rod, lift the handles of the valve cross shaft and put it into reverse. None of this, it seemed to Challoner, had the hallmark of the perfection he always sought.

He gathered up the papers and slipped them into a leather bag.

One other operation had to be planned: the elimination of Blackstone. But the success of the train robbery depended on keeping him alive. Challoner worried about this before deciding that it was a question of timing. When Blackstone's usefulness had expended itself he would kill him. He looked in the mirror again because it would be like killing himself.

Chapter Seven

The following night Blackstone returned to The Naked Man to see if there were any messages. There was one, a small package containing Sir Geoffrey Hawkins's bullet mould. Birnie you thief, Blackstone thought. The note said: "I note that what was a straightforward highway robbery has now deteriorated into a navvy murder and a riot. I trust you are making more progress than you did in your two previous assignments."

Blackstone checked his trunk to see if it had been disturbed; the strand of gossamer black silk around the lock was unbroken. He unlocked it and checked his guns and his gilt-crowned baton.

The landlord pocketed five more sovereigns and said: "What weather. Makes you wonder if it will ever end. They're rationing the water now."

"As long as they're not rationing ale," Blackstone said, thinking of the navvies who drank five quarts a day. He ordered himself a dog's nose, remembering the girl and her honeysuckle perfume. He asked the landlord about her.

"Left next morning – without as much as a thank you."

"Did she have anything to thank you for?"

"Not really. She locked the door."

Blackstone wondered if she had reached London. He felt nostalgic. He smelled the fruit in Covent Garden; heard the cries of girls selling lavender; saw the sun rising over the fields outside his home in Paddington Village. He missed the girl from the Brown Bear; he missed the company of George Ruthven and the other Runners; he missed his horse Poacher. He was tired of navvying.

He asked the landlord: "Anywhere I can make some bullets?"

The landlord pointed to the courtyard. "You'll find a brazier out there."

Blackstone took some lead, Sir Geoffrey Hawkins's mould and the ball he had taken from Frying Pan Charlie's chest. He was glad none of the other Runners were around because this was an experiment in criminal investigation and he didn't like sharing his failures.

The theory was simple. If you found a distinguishing mark on a bullet then there should be a corresponding mark in the mould in which the bullet had been made.

He melted the lead over the brazier and spooned some into the scissor-type mould. When it was cool he compared the bullet with the one which had killed Frying Pan Charlie. There had been a pimple on it, but there was no corresponding mark on the bullet he had just made. He wasn't surprised. But there were other suspects, other moulds.

"Have you only made one?" the landlord asked.

"It only takes one to kill a man," Blackstone said, staring at him.

He went upstairs and wrote a letter to a contact in Liverpool. Then, with the dog behind him, he set off for Shanty Town to find the bullet mould used by Petro, king of the navvies.

Two o'clock in the morning. The navvies had spent their delayed pay and Shanty Town was quiet except for the barking of a dog, the scutter of rats, the hooting of an owl, and the snoring of the guard who awoke occasionally with a splutter and peered around in the moonlight.

Petro was away in the village with the girl he had met on the day of the riot.

Blackstone wanted his mould. And any other evidence. In particular any evidence indicting Henry Challoner.

Challoner in front of the magistrate. Challoner sent for trial. Challoner on the gallows. The noose tightened round Blackstone's neck....

The cottage faced the field with the embankment behind it; Blackstone approached from behind. Just the one guard, sitting in front of the door with a blunderbuss across his knees and a bottle, three-quarters empty, at his feet.

Blackstone carried one of Alice's kitchen knives. He usually carried a long French dirk; but one of Alice's knives was sufficient for opening a window.

Blackstone paused and crouched at the foot of the embankment as the guard awoke. He was a big man named Geneva who distilled his own gin. He stood up, made a few flourishes with his blunderbuss, finished the liquor in the bottle and settled himself in the moonlight once more.

Blackstone ran to the cottage. He slid the blade of the knife into the window, which opened with a small, rotten sound. You could poke your finger into the thick silence inside, he thought.

He smelled stale tobacco smoke and polish. Who but Petro would use polish in Shanty Town? Perhaps the money was kept here. The money levied from the navvies. The money stolen from the stagecoach.

The window was just large enough for him to climb through. He was thankful for the moonlight. He made for the table which had a drawer facing the chair in which Petro had been sitting when they first met.

The chiming clock chimed.

Blackstone froze.

The bodyguard snored on.

Blackstone applied the knife to the drawer, slipping it up and down looking for the lock.

The blade had just found it when the blow caught him on the back of the neck. His next conscious sensation was pain.

Honeysuckle.

That was his second waking impression. Then warmth and softness. The pain persisted.

"Rookie," she said, "I didn't mean to hit you so hard."

"Why hit me at all?" He moved his head against her breasts.

"I thought you were a thief."

Blackstone struggled with his memory. After a while he said: "I thought you warned people to stay away from him."

"You didn't take any notice of the warning."

She seemed to be redirecting the conversation. "What were you doing in Petro's?" Blackstone asked.

"Waiting for him."

"Why?"

She didn't reply.

"You were his girl, weren't you?" The knowledge disappointed him. He sat up and looked around in the moonlight. They were still in Petro's place and there was a guard outside. "What about him?" he whispered, pointing at the door.

"Geneva? You needn't worry about him. He's finished for the night. Drinking his own stuff," she explained.

"Why did you come back?"

"The usual reasons," she said. "I got as far as Manchester. Then I turned back. Thanks for the gold 'un," she said, remembering the sovereign. "You shouldn't have." Her fingers found the swelling on his head; they were very gentle. "Why did you put it in my pocket?"

"So you wouldn't feel obliged to make the landlord of The Naked Man happy."

"That bastard," she said. "I'm not really as bad as you think," she said after a while.

"I only thought you were as bad as you said you were. Dolly, Molly, Polly."

"I'm not a tallywoman."

"I believe you."

"And I was never easy in the Rookery. Although it was hard enough."

"I know." The Rookery had made Blackstone a thief.

"There's only ever been Petro."

"You warned me off him."

"He's no good, that's why."

"Why did you come back then?"

"You've already asked me that."

"Do you love him?"

"I don't know," she said. "He was good to me."

"He said he beat you."

"There are worse things than a beating."

"Hitting people on the back of the head is worse."

"I thought you were a thief."

"I am," Blackstone said.

"There's nothing to pinch here," she told him. "Nothing much, anyway."

"Do you know where Petro is tonight?"

"With some woman, I suppose. Some blower," She brightened. "I don't care so much now."

"You shouldn't have come back. Petro's more than a bully." Blackstone hesitated: Petro was probably a murderer. "He's not just a magsman. You should get away while you can."

"I know what he is," the girl said.

"I don't think you do."

"He's a villain," she said. "I know what he's up to." In the moonlight the sulkiness was erased and her voice sounded very young.

"What's he up to?" Blackstone asked.

"Never you mind. You'd best keep out of it. Go thieving somewhere else." She stroked the back of his neck below the swelling. "I don't want anything to happen to you." She went on stroking, then asked: "How are your hands?" She found the bandages. "Your poor hands," she said. "I warned you."

He touched her cheek with his fingertips; her youth frightened him. He said: "I wonder what would have happened if we'd met in the Rookery."

"You wouldn't have noticed me."

"Oh yes I would," he said, although he wasn't sure because there were many Mollys there.

"Honest?"

"Honest."

"Are you going to wait here for him?" Blackstone asked.

"What else is there for me to do? Move into one of the huts and become a tallywoman?"

"You could stay in a village."

"Petro would find me." She put a cushion behind Blackstone's head and walked to the open window. "In any case it's not your worry."

But it was. Blackstone said: "I'll find you a place to stay. Then I'll take you back to London."

"Why, Rookie," she asked. "Why?"

"Because," he said.

"And what would I do when I got back to London? Go on the streets? Down the Haymarket or Windmill Street? No, Rookie, I'd best stay here."

"I'd find you a decent job," Blackstone told her.

"Why, do you fancy me or something?" Her voice was coquettish, incongruous.

Blackstone didn't reply because you couldn't tell a girl that you grieved for her and everything she represented, and there was nothing more to it than that. He stood up, wincing at the thrust of pain in his head. "What did you hit me with?"

"The butt of a pistol."

"Very professional," he said.

There was a milkiness on the skyline and the stars were vanishing. The night sounds had faded and a bird began to sing prematurely.

"We must go," Blackstone said. "Petro will be back soon."

"You go, Rookie. I'll stay."

Blackstone shook his head, tossing the pain around. "You come with me. Don't ask me where at the moment. But you're not staying here. He beat you up once, he'll do it again."

She hesitated, staring out of the window. Blackstone took the opportunity to pocket the bullet mould lying on the table.

He took her arm. "Come on, there isn't much time."

"I don't know," she said. "I didn't expect anything like this. I don't understand why you're doing it."

He climbed out of the window first and helped her down.

"Where are we going?"

"For a walk."

He collected the dog and they headed for a village five miles away in the direction of Stockton. The skyline brightened and the rim of the sun appeared, setting fire to islands of cloud.

"You kissed me once," she said.

"I know."

Her face was exhausted in the daylight; her lips smudged, her eyes shadowed. Farm labourers on their way to work looked at them curiously – navvy and tallywoman heading away from the railway with a bit of a dog behind them.

They arrived at the village at eight. Boys were sweeping the courtyards and there was a smell of baking bread on the air. Blackstone bought a hot loaf which they ate ravenously.

Then he took her to the gabled house where he had hired a post-chaise. The owner, a gaunt, muddled-looking man, looked at them suspiciously.

Blackstone took two sovereigns from his money belt and a lot of the suspicion departed. He told the man to look after the girl for a few days; there would be more sovereigns when he returned.

The girl said: "I don't know...."

Blackstone said: "I'll be back within three days."

"But why, Rookie? Why?"

He kissed her. "That's why," he said. Although it wasn't the reason at all.

He couldn't work, not with his blistered hands *and* the pain in his head. So he took the bullet from Frying Pan Charlie's chest, some lead and Petro's mould to a brazier on a deserted stretch of the railway.

He poured the molten metal into the mould and thought: one day the police forces of the world will be grateful to the Bow Street Runners for this discovery.

But first there had to be a success. The new science had to send a man to the gallows.

He took the ball out of Petro's mould and examined it. There was a small indentation there, but nothing that matched the pimple on the ball that had killed Frying Pan.

He decided to use the rest of the molten lead to make balls for his own pistols. He took one of his own moulds and poured the metal into it. When it was cool he removed the ball, noting with surprise that there was a pimple on it identical to the pimple on the ball that had killed Frying Pan Charlie.

Chapter Eight

The wedding ceremony was simple. Heathen according to Josephine Courtney. Unnecessary according to most of the navvies who saw no point in marriage with so many tallywomen and village girls available.

But it was an excuse for a celebration.

The ceremony was held in a hut housing twenty-five navvies; catering was by Pascoe who was still in business because the navvies had to eat and drink.

There were ten barrels of beer, twenty bottles of gin, a dozen loaves, joints of cold ham and hunks of cheese.

The bride was a village girl, flaxen, flushed and giggling with excitement. Her groom was a dark muscular Scot who had taken her from an Irishman during a randy. There were rumours that the Irish, working at the other end of the line, would try to wreck the wedding.

Outside the hut, navvies armed with cudgels stood guard.

Petro was officiating.

Blackstone gazed contemplatively at Josephine Courtney. So far she had held two open-air services with moderate congregations; she had been jubilant about it – until today; the wedding, she proclaimed, denied everything she had been trying to teach them.

Petro joined Blackstone. "What," he asked, "are we going to do about her?"

Blackstone shrugged.

"I admire her spirit," Petro said. He wore his best clothes; moleskin trousers dark and glossy, waistcoat as bright as a kingfisher's feathers. "In fact," he remarked, "she's an attractive woman."

Blackstone looked at Petro with surprise. "Is she?"

"She's got class," Petro said.

Blackstone felt he should warn the missionary. "But we've got to stop her now or she'll spoil the wedding."

And undermine your authority, Blackstone thought. He said: "You'd better lock her up."

Petro grinned. "No," he said, "you'd better lock her up. If you're going to be one of my bodyguards, you'll have to prove yourself."

"I didn't think I had to guard the king of the navvies against a woman missionary."

Petro ignored him. "Treat her gently, Rookie. I've got some ideas about that lady."

Blackstone was suddenly very tired of the assignment. Tired of navvying, tired of taking orders from a thug wearing an ear-ring. But there was Challoner: he couldn't quit. One day, culley, he thought, staring at Petro.

The navvies cleared the centre of the hut and put a broomstick on the floor.

Josephine Courtney pushed her way into the hut, face registering determination. She stood next to Blackstone and her anger reached him. "It's disgusting," she said.

He said: "May I have a word with you?"

"I've got to stop this."

"It won't start for five minutes. Come outside for a minute." He took her arm. "If you still want to come back after what I've told you I won't stop you."

"All right," she said; and they went into the sunshine. Blackstone wasn't sure what he was going to say.

"Well?" Her hair was parted in the centre, falling into ringlets at the sides; it looked very soft in the sunlight and Blackstone thought it would smell of honey.

He found his Nathaniel Mills box and took some snuff.

"A disgusting habit," she said.

"Then I'll give it up, ma'am."

"Don't make fun of me," she warned. "Say what you've got to say."

"It's just this," he said, wondering what he was launching himself upon. "That wedding – for want of a better word – will take place whether you like it or not."

"Then you don't know me, Rookie."

He held up his hand. "Please, give me a minute. That ceremony is going to take place. You can't stop it, I can't stop it. If I could I would because it lacks spiritual guidance." He dodged her gaze for a moment. "If you try and stop it you'll lose the trust of the navvies. And believe me, Josephine" – time to dispense with ma'ams – "you have gained their respect. I've been doing quite a lot of persuading on your behalf," he lied. "Your next congregation will be the biggest you've had. Don't spoil everything by trying to stop this little affair."

She thought about it, rustling the gold-leafed pages of her worn Bible. "But I can't let them go through with it. It's ... it's pagan."

"Listen," Blackstone said. "There are a lot of girls sleeping with men who aren't their husbands in Shanty Town."

She frowned.

Blackstone said: "I'm sorry, but it's a fact. You know, so there's no point in beating about the bush. At least this couple are going through some sort of a wedding. At least they're recognizing some sort of union." He spoke more urgently. "This is what you must do, Josephine. When it's all over, take them aside and suggest a proper Church wedding. What an achievement that would be. You could even get a clergyman down here to marry them." He paused. "I can see the report now in *The Navigator*: Thanks to the crusading efforts of Miss Josephine Courtney...."

"It would be an achievement," she agreed. Her face was gentle. "Do you really think it's possible, Rookie?"

"Of course it's possible."

"Very well, I won't interfere. Providing you do something for me."

Blackstone didn't like the sound of it. "What's that?"

"I've already told you. Get Petro on my side. They'll do anything he says."

Blackstone said: "I think he's already on your side."

"He hasn't done anything for me," she said.

"I rather think he's planning to," Blackstone said.

"I must get close to him," she said.

Blackstone didn't reply.

"There's just one thing," she said, as a cheer came from inside the hut. "Supposing the bridegroom's a Presbyterian, I can't get him married in my Church then."

"Then convert him," Blackstone said.

They walked back to the hut. Petro was speaking, marrying. "Now jump over the broomstick," he ordered.

The couple jumped.

And as they hurried towards the bed at the end of the hut to consummate the marriage in the presence of the navvies Blackstone hastily closed the door and said to Josephine Courtney: "Now there's something I want you to do for me."

But he didn't have time to tell her what it was. Nor was the marriage consummated immediately. Because, as the couple got into bed, the Irish arrived.

❧ ❧ ❧

The battle was short and fierce. A victory for Shanty Town. A few tough navvies got past the ambush laid by Petro and, armed with fairground livetts, reached the nuptials. But they were a spent force by then.

Blackstone took Josephine Courtney to safety. When he returned the fight was almost over.

Five Irish lay unconscious on the ground. Four others were still fighting, but finally they went down.

"Good fighters," Yankee Tom observed. His knuckles were bleeding.

"Not bad," Blackstone agreed. "And in a way they won." He pointed at the bridegroom who was lying on the ground, with a bruise on his temple.

Blackstone took Josephine Courtney back to her village to tell her what she had to do. In one village he now knew a navvy king's mistress: in another a missionary.

He took her to a coffee house with a bow-window where the landed gentry met. The coffee was roasting in the window, filling the place with beautiful burned fumes.

The owner was a plump, white-haired man with a lot of broken blood-vessels on his face. He treated the gentry with servility and anyone lower with contempt; it was incomprehensible to him that anyone with less than three servants should enter his establishment. He ignored Blackstone because navvies didn't exist at all.

Blackstone beckoned him and said cheerfully: "Coffee for two, please."

"What?" The owner focused his eyes on him.

Blackstone spelled it out. "Coffee. For two."

Finally the owner said: "If you like to go round the back the staff will find you something."

Blackstone said: "Blessed are the meek...."

"... for they shall seek God," Josephine Courtney said.

"I beg your pardon." The owner was dazed.

"Coffee for two, please."

The owner recovered his authority. "I'm afraid we don't serve navvies on these premises."

"How would you like two hundred navvies here within the hour?"

The owner said he wouldn't, and he would call a constable if Blackstone didn't get out.

The girl said: "I'm a missionary."

He looked at her with disbelief.

She took out her Bible and showed it to him. "Do you go to church regularly?" she asked.

"Not too often," he said.

"Then you must come to my services. You'll have to join the navvies in the congregation. But we're all the same in the eyes of God."

But not in the eyes of the owner. He said to Blackstone: "Get out, you. I don't want your sort of banditti round here."

Blackstone sighed. He put his rusty pistol on the table and stood up. "Please," he said. "Coffee for two. Otherwise I shall personally recommend your establishment to every navvy on the line and I'm sure your customers won't appreciate that." He glanced at the phaeton that had drawn up bringing a couple of titles out for their morning coffee.

The owner brought them coffee. "Just drink it and get out," he said. "Don't bother to pay."

Blackstone grinned at her. "Not even you can make him follow in the paths of righteousness."

She said: "You know, sometimes you don't sound like a navvy at all."

"I wasn't always a navvy. You heard me tell Petro that my last resting place was the House of Correction."

"What were you in prison for?"

"Stealing," Blackstone said. He leaned forward, enjoying the steam from the coffee pot. "That's why I want you to help me."

She sipped her coffee, eyes kind through the steam. "Can't God help you, Rookie?"

"Not in this case," Blackstone said, adding hastily: "Well, perhaps he can – through you."

She liked this.

"You see," he explained, "the man you saw that night, the highwayman, that's my brother." He put his finger to his lips. "I know what you're thinking. That the whole family must be rotten."

"Well," she said, "one thief and one highwayman...."

Blackstone leaned back in his chair. "That's what I wanted to tell you about. I didn't steal anything. I went to prison for my brother."

She poured them more coffee.

"I want you to help me find him," Blackstone said.

"I don't understand."

The other customers stared at them with hostility. A few had left already. A navvy wasn't good for business.

Blackstone explained that his brother had been twice convicted for thieving. Once as a youth for smatter hauling – stealing handkerchiefs – and once for hoisting, stealing from shops. A third conviction would have got him transported for life or sent to the gallows. "So I took his place," Blackstone explained. "No one ever guessed."

Her face was shining. "That was a marvellous thing to do, Rookie. I knew you were different from the others. But why are you working as a navigator?"

"I've got to earn a living. A job's not easy to come by after you've been inside."

She touched his bandaged hands. Bandaged hands seemed to have an appeal, Blackstone thought.

"Now you already know what my brother looks like," Blackstone said.

She nodded. "Just like you. Except that he limps. Mind you, he had a mask on. But I can see the family likeness."

"You see," Blackstone went on, "there's only two of us. My mother's a widow...."

"Why do you want to find him, Rookie? It seems to me that you should let him go his own way."

"That's not a very Christian attitude," he said.

"No, I suppose not."

"Now he's started thieving again and I thought perhaps if I could get to him.... I don't want to go inside again for him, so you see my motives aren't entirely selfless. Perhaps if you could have a word with him. You're a very persuasive lady."

"Only because I have HIM behind me." She indicated the blue sky distorted by the bottle-glass windows. "But tell me something, Rookie, why can't you find him?"

"Because," Blackstone said, "I must work and earn some money. Some honest money," he emphasized. "I can't afford to waste time looking for my brother." He paused. "Did you notice which direction he took after he had robbed the stage?"

She nodded. "He rode off towards Stockton. It might have been my imagination but I thought I saw a horseman heading back in the opposite direction some time later. Just a figure on the skyline. But it was moonlight. Perhaps it was just my fancy."

"No, it wasn't your fancy. That's exactly what he would have done. It's my guess he would have gone back to Darlington. That's what I would have done."

"I beg your pardon?"

"I wonder," he asked, "is there any chance that you'll be going to Darlington within the next few days?"

"As a matter of fact," she said, "I'm going tomorrow. I have to collect the latest edition of *The Navigator*."

"Then you could keep a look-out for him." Alarm spurted inside him. "But please don't approach him." He thought desperately. "We'll do that together."

She smiled understandingly.

Where would Challoner stay? Not in a tavern. Nowhere where he might attract attention. Some quiet room that had been advertised recently. Above a shop, perhaps. Off the main street. Near a stables. Darlington wasn't all that big. Whatever Blackstone would have done Challoner would have done: that was the way it had always been.

He drained his coffee and advised her where to look.

"Don't forget your part of the bargain," she reminded him. "Get Petro to support me. Get the men to my services. Get them to buy *The Navigator*. Then we've got that wedding to look forward to."

"Ah yes," Blackstone said, "the wedding."

"Don't work too hard, Rookie." She touched his hands again.

"I won't." He stood up and the coffee shop became quiet. He bowed and stuck the pistol back in his belt. "Not bad coffee," he said in a loud voice. "Better than the tommy shops." He told the owner: "Actually I'm one of George III's bastard sons."

Josephine Courtney didn't hear him. "Isn't it marvellous," she said, "the two of us going about God's work together."

Except that I'm about the devil's work, Blackstone thought.

First she checked with the printers that her *Navigators* were ready. Then she carried out her part of the bargain, inquiring at the sort of places Rookie had suggested for a man who looked like him. A man with his build, his presence; a man whose eyes had glittered behind a mask, a highwayman who walked with a limp.

She walked the streets of Darlington for two hours, silencing mouchers, beggars, footpads and local blades with her tongue and the Bible.

She was quite tired when she spotted him. It was the limp that identified him. Then the shoulders, the walk, the way other pedestrians got out of his way.

She followed him at a distance of a hundred yards.

Once he stopped, swivelled and stared down the street. She handed a one-eyed pedlar selling ballad sheets about the Stockton and Darlington a copy of *The Navigator* and engaged him in animated conversation of which he didn't comprehend a word.

The highwayman appeared satisfied and walked on.

She followed him until he turned into the doorway of a chandler's shop.

CHAPTER NINE

The date was 13 September 1825.
In Newcastle, George Stephenson, who had called in the Bow Street Runners, wrote a letter.

It said: "The improved travelling engine was tried here last night and fully answered my expectations, and if you will be kind enough to desire Pickersgill to send horses to take it away from here on Friday it shall be loaded on Thursday evening."

It was just under three years and four months earlier that Thomas Meynell, chairman of the new railway company, had laid the first piece of the S and D at St John's Crossing, Stockton.

The scenes were described as the most flamboyant since Waterloo. Flags, bunting, drinking, bands, cannons firing and Meynell transported on a carriage pulled by singing navvies.

Meynell laid the line without speaking, enabling vendors in the crowd to sell blank sheets of paper entitled "A full and Faithful Report of What Mr Meynell said at the Opening".

13 September. Fourteen days until the opening of the world's first public steam locomotion railway.

In the Newcastle factory in Forth Street Stephenson patted the smokestack of his gawky travelling engine,

Locomotion. She had to succeed for the sake of his son, Robert, for the sake of railways, for the sake of the future, for the sake of George Stephenson, who had come from nothing only to be treated as a foreigner by the politicians. For every mile of cutting wrecked by storms, for every marsh covered; for every threat, for every sneer, for every act of violence. He remembered his own words over a bottle of wine in a Stockton tavern. "I venture to tell you that I think you will live to see the day when railways will supersede almost all other methods of conveyance in this country." He had added in his thick accent that he hoped he would live to see the day. And he would, God willing. What's more he would drive Locomotion during the trials and at the opening. Provided the boiler didn't burst and the wheels held and the Bow Street Runner kept the peace.

In his Gothic home on the same day Sir Joshua Eccleston presided at a dinner which fell just short of being a banquet. There was a lot of money and prestige represented, including members of the Pease family who had backed the new railway. It was the sort of occasion Sir Joshua enjoyed. "Gentlemen," he said, after they had toasted the King, "the first locomotive is due to leave Newcastle in three days' time. May God be with her." His words were followed by the murmur of assent to which Sir Joshua was accustomed. If God *was* with Locomotion then a prosperous future was assured for Sir Joshua. He didn't voice these sentiments because they were hardly suitable for an after-dinner speech.

Sir Geoffrey Hawkins took his wine with Lord Derby, Lord Sefton, Lord Eldon, Lord Darlington and the canal owner, Bradshaw – all stalwarts of the opposition to railways. He would have liked to share his plans for the S and D with them. But it was too risky; they were too orthodox. So he sipped his wine and let them chat in their defeatist way about the forthcoming opening without confiding in them. Without telling them that it would never open.

In the room above the chandler's in Darlington, Henry Challoner put the final touches to his plan to kill Edmund Blackstone after the Bow Street Runner had served his purpose. In his bunk in The Rectory, Blackstone, armed with the address in Darlington supplied by Josephine Courtney, made his plans to eliminate Challoner.

Two women thought a lot about Blackstone that evening.

The girl called Molly as she ate a meal of cold meat and pickles, watched suspiciously by the owner of the post-chaise and his grey, listless wife.

Josephine Courtney as she checked her small pocket pistol and her dagger. And later, just before retiring, as she stood naked in front of a long mirror, touching her breasts and running her hands down her thighs.

Plan Two
The Wrecking

Chapter One

Blackstone went looking for Challoner one evening after a sombre day working on the embankment. A navvy had been killed by a derailed truck and, in The Rectory, the men remembered: six navvies buried when a canal tunnel caved in; an explosion killing two and maiming one when someone knocked out his pipe in a keg of gunpowder; a cutting known as the slaughterhouse, so great was its toll of life.

It was a brooding evening and there were bruises on the horizon; it looked as if the weather was at last going to break.

Blackstone checked the old pistol. He would have to buy another in Darlington because it wasn't a fitting executioner for Challoner.

Yankee Tom asked: "Where are you off to?"

"A girl," Blackstone said.

"With a barker?"

"She's got a husband."

"You don't have to bother with the married ones, Rookie."

Blackstone shrugged.

Yankee Tom said: "I hear Petro's taken a shine to the missionary."

"Each to his own," Blackstone said.

"What are you up to?" Yankee Tom asked.

"I told you."

"Sure you told me." Yankee Tom chewed a fresh plug of tobacco. "But you're no navvy. Never were."

"You've got to start sometime," Blackstone said. He checked his money-belt and pulled on his boots.

Yankee Tom spat into his spittoon, a biscuit tin. He said: "If I were you I'd clear out."

"Why?"

"Because you're making too many enemies and bad friends."

"You mean Petro?"

"He'll do for you, Rookie, because he thinks you're dangerous. You're a threat to him."

"Maybe I am."

"Don't say I haven't warned you."

Blackstone grinned at the American. "I won't. And thanks," he added, sticking the gun into his belt.

"She must be quite a girl."

"She is."

He raised his hand in a salute and walked past Alice's creaking chair into the brooding evening. The contused clouds were approaching and thunder grumbled in the distance. He tied up the dog and set off for some stables where he could hire a horse and ride to Darlington.

The Gorger allowed him a three-minute start before following.

The horse was a grey which had known better times and forgotten them long ago. But it was a friendly animal and Blackstone stroked its neck as they travelled together.

A few blobs of rain fell. When they hit the dust a thirsty smell arose. Lightning flickered on the skyline.

On the outskirts of Darlington Blackstone tethered the horse outside a gunsmith's.

The gunsmith, a small, bright man with fingers twitching for a trigger, tried to sell Blackstone a Brown Bess. "Forty-six-inch barrel," he said. "The weapon of the British infantry," as if that sealed the matter.

Blackstone said: "I want a pistol that shoots straight, not a dangerous, worn-out old barker manufactured in 1720."

The gunsmith stared at him indignantly. "The Brown Bess is still very much in use," he said. Adequate for a navvy, he implied.

Blackstone said: "What have you got in the way of percussion."

"As a matter of fact," the gunsmith said, "we do have a fowling piece by Fuller of Wardour Street."

"You mean George Fuller of 104 Wardour Street?" Blackstone shook his head. "I don't like his guns." He examined the gunsmith's stock with resignation. "I suppose I shall have to settle for a conversion."

The gunsmith said resentfully: "What do you want it for?"

"To kill someone."

The gunsmith said: "I think I'd better...."

"You'd better do nothing," Blackstone told him. "What do you think guns are for? To tickle people with?" He spotted a twin-barrelled conversion by Barber of Newark. A wicked gun with a tiny sight between its shiny barrels. "How much?"

"More than a navigator can afford," the gunsmith said.

"Twenty guineas?"

"Twenty-five."

Blackstone opened his money belt and tossed fifteen guineas on the mahogany counter. "Give it to me."

"I said twenty-five."

"Give it to me," Blackstone said softly. "And everything that goes with it. It's a fair price. There are some bullets?"

The gunsmith nodded.

"Good." Blackstone took the gun. It wasn't the best, he thought. It would never be the pride of his collection. But good enough to kill Challoner. He tried out the mechanism. "It'll do."

"Take it then," the gunsmith said. "But don't tell me who you're going to kill."

"Gunsmiths never want to know that," Blackstone said.

Rain was falling heavily, thunder and lightning catching up with it.

Blackstone left the horse under an archway and waited in a doorway opposite the chandler's. It was dusk and lights from windows held the falling rain and lit shining pools on the cobblestones.

Horsemen galloped home to dinner, their cloaks streaming heavily in the rain. Those without horses, and, perhaps, homes, took the rain badly, cringing along the street, clothes and hair plastered against their bodies.

Lightning lit the street, followed by a crack of thunder. Blackstone was happy with the storm because a gunshot could be mistaken for thunder.

He waited until it was almost dark, justifying what he was going to do. Challoner was wanted for several murders; he was also wanted for his part in the Cato Street Conspiracy – their first meeting, when Blackstone, the newest Runner, had chased and lost him. In theory it was Blackstone's duty to arrest Challoner and bring him to trial. But you didn't keep men like Challoner in custody because they didn't stay there.

If Challoner had been at home a candle or a lamp would have been lit by now; but the rooms were in darkness. Blackstone ran across the glistening cobblestones, as slippery as fish-scales, and pressed himself into the alley beside the chandler's.

To reach Challoner's room he had to go through the shop which was locked up. He took housekeeping tools from his pocket – picklocks and an "outsider" pair of pliers for grasping the tip of a key through a lock – and worked on the door; it took longer than usual because his hands were cold and wet and blistered. After five minutes the door opened. He closed it gently.

The shop smelled of oil and candles and vermin. A clock ticked noisily on the wall. Lightning flashed, printing a picture of the shop in Blackstone's mind. He made his way to a door behind the counter hoping that the cat which all shopkeepers kept wasn't around.

He climbed the winding stairs carefully, but each step answered him with a creak. He paused outside Challoner's room, listening. He tried the handle of the door with little hope and found to his surprise that it opened. He pushed the door abruptly, standing back, cocked pistol in his hand. Nothing.

Lightning filled the room. A bookcase, table and chairs, sofa, stuffed owl in a glass case given transient life by the lightning. Blackstone went in.

For a moment he stood there, feeling Challoner's personality in the thick silence between the thunder. He knew where Challoner slept, which chair he used, how he stood at the window gazing down the street, because that was the way it would have been with him.

He sat down at the table on which there was a sheet of paper. He gazed at it intently. He couldn't be sure, not until the lightning helped him. This time the lightning was overhead, the flash brighter than daylight. He hadn't been wrong: one word was written on the sheet of paper: BLACKSTONE.

In the corner the owl winked in the explosion of light.

Blackstone put his pistol on the table. How the hell did Challoner know he was around? Someone who knew he was operating under cover must have told him. Who?

Blackstone went to the window and stared at the rain sweeping down the main street, exploding on the cobblestones, washing away summer.

"Makes you think, doesn't it, Blackie?" Challoner said from the doorway.

Challoner held a pistol in each hand. He pointed to a chair beside the table. "Sit down, Blackie. It's a long time since we had a chat." He put down one pistol and, with his free hand, lit a candle-lantern. "In fact we've never had a really good talk. Just a few words all those years ago when we were on the same side of the law." He swept Blackstone's pistol off the table.

Blackstone sat down. "How did you know I was here?"

"Easy, culley. We both think the same way, don't we? So when I see a young missionary lady who's been in your company following me down the street I know it's only a matter of time before Edmund Blackstone, the great Bow Street Runner, comes sniffing around. And what better time than tonight with all that thunder and lightning? A good night for a killing, eh, Blackie?"

Blackstone said: "How did you know I had met the missionary?"

Challoner said: "That would be telling, Blackie."

"Does it matter if you're going to kill me?"

"That sort of thing always matters, Blackie. It would be peaching, wouldn't it? I never liked a nose, you know that." Lightning lit his harsh face, finding its hollows. "I also feel very strongly about bastards who go over to the other side and use the knowledge they picked up in the Rookery to put their less fortunate friends behind bars."

Blackstone wanted to tell him about the sort of criminal he enjoyed putting behind bars. Flashmen putting children on the streets; landlords cramming paupers into doss houses until they suffocated; blackmailers; Society sadists and perverts; every hypocrite living off others' poverty. But he didn't because he couldn't apologize to Challoner.

"So what are you going to do?" Blackstone asked. He considered pushing the table over; it wouldn't work but it would be a last gesture.

"Kill you, of course."

"Then get on with it."

"I want to savour the moment. It had to come some day, didn't it, Blackie? You or me."

"How did you get up here? I would have heard the stairs creaking."

"I was already here. Out in the corridor. But you were too hasty, Blackie. Too keen to get into my room and surprise me. What were you going to do? Take me back to Bow Street? Birnie would have been very proud of you. From stealing wipes to catching notorious criminals. Very commendable."

"You could have done the same," Blackstone said, "if you'd wanted to."

Challoner leaned across the table, his voice acrid. "That's just the point, isn't it. I didn't want to. I prefer to be a genuine villain, not a criminal protected by a baton with a crown on it. Because there isn't much difference in what we do, is there Blackie? Set a thief to catch a thief. Have you ever taken brass from a cracksman? A little for him, a little for you and the balance back to the victim?"

Blackstone had, every Bow Street Runner had.

Challoner said: "Is that any different from us ordinary criminals?"

"Perhaps not." Challoner was asserting what he had often felt.

"Except," Challoner said, "that you're protected by the law. Wave your little baton and all things are possible, eh, Blackie?" Blackstone shrugged.

Challoner said: "I want one thing before I kill you, Blackie."

"What's that?"

"Your baton, culley. Your beautiful baton with the crown on it. Symbol of law and order. It would serve me well."

Blackstone put his hands on the edge of the table. It was possible that he might catch Challoner off balance; but not very likely. He shook his head. "You'll never get that."

"Bow Street Runners always carry their batons."

"Not when they're disguised as members of the banditti. The dangerous class."

Challoner drummed his angers on the table before asking: "Where is it?"

"You don't expect me to tell you. Would you tell me if the situations were reversed?"

Challoner relaxed a little. "No, I suppose not. That's always been our trouble, hasn't it – we know each other too well. I wonder...."

"I've often wondered, too," Blackstone said, because he knew Challoner was debating their birthright.

They stared at each other in the candle-light.

Blackstone said quietly: "Why don't you get on with it?"

"Don't worry, culley. I'll do what I've got to do."

Blackstone tensed himself. Then he heard a stair creak. Challoner stood up, pointing the barrel of a pistol at Blackstone's chest. "Any last requests?" He took a pace backwards. "The end of a partnership in a way."

You couldn't really blame the Gorger, Blackstone thought much later. When he burst into the room he could see only one man. Challoner silhouetted against the window. And there was no difference between the silhouettes of Challoner and Blackstone.

The Gorger hit the door with his shoulder and clubbed at Challoner's neck with the butt of a pistol.

But Challoner's reactions had been finely honed in the jungle that is the Rookery. He swung round, catching the blow on his shoulder. As he turned he fired the pistol and the ball smashed the window. The flame of the candle fluttered like a trapped moth.

Blackstone dived for his own pistol on the floor. By now the Gorger was thoroughly confused. He hadn't bargained with two Rookies. He aimed his pistol first at one, then the other. He kicked the pistol out of Blackstone's reach and swung with his other foot at Challoner. Challoner took the kick in the kidneys; rolled away towards the door.

The Gorger shouted: "Stay where you are." Challoner stopped; so did Blackstone. The armed man was between them. "Which of you is Rookie?"

"He is," Blackstone yelled. He tackled the Gorger knee high, bringing him down. The Gorger fell, one arm knocking the candle-lantern over the sofa. The flame hesitated, then skipped joyfully over the upholstery. Thick smoke rolled across the room.

Dimly, Blackstone saw Challoner standing at the door, one arm hanging uselessly at his side. In the other hand he held a bag. Blackstone found his double-barrelled pistol and fired at Challoner; the ball punched out a panel of the door.

The flames cracked the owl's glass cage and devoured its occupant.

The Gorger was trying to get up, coughing and pulling at the handkerchief knotted at his neck. Blackstone butted him in the belly, hearing the air hiss from his lungs, and made for the door. He heard the door downstairs crash. He ran down the stairs into the street and saw a fleeing figure blurred by the steady rain. He loosed off the second barrel, but the figure didn't hesitate.

Blackstone thought about getting his horse and pursuing. But, above him, flames were leaping out of the window. Within seconds they would reach the oil and candles and the shop would be devoured in one hungry sheet of flame.

He ran up the stairs and pulled the Gorger's heavy body out of the smoke. Holding him under the shoulders, he dragged him down the stairs, into the street.

A crowd was gathering, calling for buckets of water. The fire brigade was said to be on its way.

"Must have been the lightning," someone said.

Blackstone left the Gorger sitting in the gutter coughing up smoke. The chandler's was gutted but the firemen, helped by the rain, thought they could save the adjoining buildings.

Blackstone patted the frightened horse and spoke to it gently. Why, he wondered, had Challoner delayed so long with the execution? And why did I miss Challoner framed in the doorway?

Chapter Two

But the storm was only an interlude. The sun emerged again, wanly at first, then gaining strength, sucking the moisture back from the earth. Green shoots, encouraged by the deluge, were burned back and the countryside reverted to straw.

The navvies were shoring up the last embankment. They worked energetically, anticipating the last big payout, the celebration party at the end of the job, the last randy.

Blackstone worked hard, watched closely by the gang boss, an ex-prizefighter called Hopkins, who had decided he was a shirker. Shovelling earth into a barrow with his short, knife-edged spade, Blackstone tried to work out a programme which would allow him to fulfil all his engagements without making Hopkins suspicious.

He had to meet Birnie at Skerne Bridge to report progress – an unsolved murder in which his own gun had been used and an encounter with Challoner who had escaped; Molly had sent an urgent message asking him to meet her; Petro had ordered him to meet him in the Fighting Cocks tavern.

Blackstone put down his shovel and climbed up the embankment to the track where Hopkins watched his men like a gaoler watching convicts breaking stones.

"Yes," Hopkins said, "what is it?" His thick forearms were folded across his chest; his broken face always a little dazed.

Blackstone said: "I've got to go and see Petro."

"You're seeing no one." His eyes were cushioned by puffy scar-tissue. "You've been away too often."

"I've got to go," Blackstone said.

"If you go, culley, you go for ever."

One or two navvies leaned on their shovels, listening with interest.

"Listen," Hopkins said, "I'm here to make bloody sure this railway gets finished. I'm responsible to the contractor and if I don't get the work done I'm out of a job."

"Pascoe? You're not frightened of him, are you?"

"I'm frightened of no one," the gang boss said. "Least of all you." He massaged his misshapen knuckles.

"Not even Petro?"

"Not even him."

"Because it's him you'll be dealing with."

"I can take care of him."

"Shall I tell him that?"

"Tell him what you like."

Blackstone threw down his shovel. "I'm going to see him." He waited a moment but the gang boss didn't move. Blackstone felt sorry for him, for what the man might have been before pickled fists took their toll. But there wasn't any doubt who held the power. Petro was stronger than the gang boss, stronger than the contractor. At what level did his power fade?

The girl was waiting for him on a seat on the village green. A procession of ducks made their way to what was left of the pond and doves perched in the dusty sycamore trees like plump white fruit.

She looked better now, he thought, with colour in her cheeks and a new softness to her features. A happy girl keeping a lover's tryst, the spectres of poverty temporarily banished. But as he approached, he realized that she was scared.

"Rookie." She stood up. Her eagerness warmed him; he felt almost paternal.

He kissed her. "You're looking fine," he said.

She didn't waste any time. "Petro's been here," she said.

"When?"

"Yesterday."

"How did he find you?"

"Someone must have seen me here. I was quite well known in Shanty Town...."

"The queen of the navvies?" Blackstone grinned at her.

"Either that or your friend the landlord peached."

"I doubt it. He's had a few yellow boys off me and he knows there's more where they came from. What did Petro want?"

"He wanted me back."

"And are you going?"

"I don't know, Rookie."

High up in the trees the doves made soothing noises.

"I told you I'd find you a job in London."

"As a chambermaid? A dollymop?"

"No," Blackstone said. "Something else." He tried to think what.

"I'd like to believe you, Rookie. I really would." She moved closer to him on the bench. The countryside drowsed around them. The ducks reached the pond and paddled in, crowding the surface shrunk by the drought. She said: "But what could you do? I don't want to hurt your feelings, Rookie, really I don't. But what could a tea-leaf" – she used rhyming slang to soften the truth – "do for me?"

"Did Petro get rough?" Blackstone wanted time to sort it out. Did you tell a navvy king's mistress, a girl you'd met by accident in a tavern, that you weren't what you seemed? No, he decided – there was a limit to mistakes.

"Not really. He just threatened me." She fingered the collar of her blue dress with its leg-o'-mutton sleeves. "But he said he'd be back."

"Did you mention me?"

"Of course I didn't. He'd kill you if he found out."

"Maybe it would be the other way round."

She shook her head. "He's got his bodyguards."

"I may become one of them."

She ignored him. "They'd beat you up and pretend it had happened in a fight. The law doesn't take much notice of navvies getting killed."

"Or shoot me like Frying Pan Charlie?"

She looked at him blankly.

He said: "So you're going back?"

"What else is there for me to do?"

"I've told you."

She was silent for a moment. A shepherd drove a herd of cows with swollen udders past. On the other side of the green small boys threw sticks into a horse chestnut tree to dislodge conkers. "Could you really see me all right in London, Rookie?"

He nodded.

She moved closer. "It's very sweet of you." Her voice fell to a whisper. "Perhaps I could help. If you really mean it."

"Help?"

"You haven't got much brass have you, Rookie? I mean if you had you wouldn't be working here, would you." She was very knowing and very young at the same time. "I know where you got those sovereigns from. You pinched them, didn't you? Or sold what you pinched at a jerryshop." She was proud of her perception.

"I'm not rich," Blackstone told her truthfully.

"Do you want to know how to make some blunt?"

Blackstone listened warily.

She was wary, too. "You wouldn't let on to Petro?"

"Is it likely?"

"No," she said. "I suppose not."

"What is it, Molly?"

"Would there be a big reward for information that would stop the railway being wrecked?"

Blackstone's pulse accelerated. "A big reward, I should think. Why, were you going to wreck it?" He laughed to disguise the excitement in his voice.

"Petro is."

"How do you know?"

"I suppose I've known for some time. He got drunk once and talked about it. But only vaguely. I didn't understand. Then yesterday he was boasting a bit. Telling me why I should stick with him because of all the money that was coming his way."

"What money?"

"Apparently there are a lot of rich swells backing him. Landowners and canal owners and the like. There's been a lot of talk about the harm the railway will do, hasn't there, Rookie?"

"It's been in the papers," Blackstone told her.

"I can't read," she said; and he was sorry. She went on: "Anyway, I've been trying to remember what I heard the first time. It seems these gentlemen are prepared to spend a lot of brass to get the Stockton and Darlington wrecked." She paused, concentrating. "And there was talk of this new railway they're thinking of building from Liverpool to Manchester. They reckon it all depends on this one. If anything happens to the S and D then they won't go ahead with the other. Is this all making sense to you?" she asked Blackstone.

He squeezed her arm. "It's making a lot of sense."

"Good," she said, "because it's all a bit above my head."

"Any names?"

She looked puzzled.

"Did they mention any of the swells who were putting up the money?"

"Not that I can remember," she said. "Does it matter?"

"It would help if we could give a few names when we go and collect the reward."

She nodded wisely. "I'll try and remember."

"How are they going to wreck it?"

"I don't know. All I know is, they're going to try and make it look natural – so that people will say the railways are unsafe."

"Where are they going to do it?"

"I don't know," she said. "Surely it's enough to tell a constable that they're going to try and wreck it."

A dog barked and some crows flew from the elm trees, flying high in the sky until they looked like scraps of charred paper.

Blackstone considered the possibilities. The obvious target was Locomotion. There was, for instance, the Stephenson safety-valve. If you tied the arm of the valve down there was a fair chance that there would be an explosion powerful enough to kill the driver. George Stephenson, perhaps.

Or a fire started in the desert-dry fields. Just what the enemies of steam had always forecast. All it would need would be two or three men with tinder boxes – and flying cinders would immediately be blamed.

Blackstone said: "We can't go to the authorities with information as vague as this. Is there any way you can find out more?"

"You mean see Petro again?"

"No," Blackstone said, "I suppose not."

She looked as if she might cry.

"No, of course not," he said. When she had recovered he asked: "Who were the other men involved?"

"Three of his bodyguards," she said.

"Is that all?"

"And Pascoe."

"But Petro half-killed him the other day." Blackstone related the episode with the watered ale. "He wouldn't do that if Pascoe was in the plot – Pascoe would peach on him."

"I doubt it." She found a handkerchief and dabbed at her eyes. "For one thing he's too scared of Petro. And for another he'd lose his cut. I gather it's pretty big," she added.

"Look," Blackstone said, "I want you to stay here a little while."

"And get beaten up by Petro."

"I'll look after Petro."

She didn't believe him and Blackstone didn't blame her.

He gave her another couple of sovereigns from his money belt. "Look, get a coach to The Naked Man and hide up there for a while. Tell the landlord I sent you and he'll have to answer to me."

"Why should he?"

"Never mind. Let's just say I've got him worried."

"Scared stiff by the sound of it. No, Rookie, I'll stay here. Lock myself in. I'll be all right. She watched the crows settling again. "Then you didn't mean it – about me getting more information out of Petro?"

"Do you think I'd allow him to get near you any more?"

"I don't know," she said.

"You'll have to believe me," he said.

"I believe you," she said.

He stood up. "One last thing. Did they say when all this was going to happen?"

"Oh yes," she said. "They're having some trials or something, aren't they?"

Blackstone nodded.

"That's when it's going to happen."

On his way back Blackstone noticed handbills fluttering on trees, doors, fences. Farm workers stared at him impassively when he stopped to read one. It said:

Less than a week to go. On Sept. 27 your future will be settled. If the Stockton and Darlington Railway is allowed to open prepare yourself for the poorhouse.

The handbill elaborated in the usual way. Cornfields razed, cattle dying, hens not laying. Work taken from the horses who would no longer need oats and hay. "Are you going to stand by and let this happen? Are you going to allow the Stockton and Darlington to open?"

It was, Blackstone decided, a clear case of incitement.

But the handbills worried him for another reason which he could not determine. Some instinct that had been nurtured inside him since he became a Runner.

He stopped and looked at another poster. There was something familiar about it.

He ran his finger along the letters, stopping at the first large *t*. The bottom of the type was broken off so that the letter looked more like a crucifix.

He had seen a similar *t* somewhere before; but he couldn't remember where.

❧ ❧ ❧

They ate chickens – one each – poached from farms and tankards of hock stolen from a mansion.

They were in the back room of the Fighting Cocks. At the head of the table sat Petro in his full navvy regalia. He was smoking a cigar from which he had bitten a butt as large as a thumbnail.

Two bodyguards sat on one side of him, big men with jowels greasy from chicken fat. They hardly spoke, concentrating on the steaming meat and the hock which they drank like beer.

On the other side sat the third henchman, a former butcher, bearded and flushed, and Pascoe the contractor. He looked nervous.

Blackstone sat at the far end of the table facing Petro. He was thinking that, as Challoner knew about his disguise, it was possible that everyone in the room shared the knowledge.

Petro said: "I hope you enjoy our little celebration. We meet here once a fortnight." He stared down the table. "I suppose some people might wonder which of us is at the head of the table. What do you think, Rookie?"

"You're the king," Blackstone said.

"I'm glad you think so." Petro paused. "Miss Courtney speaks very highly of you." He gnawed at a chicken leg. "And so do one or two other people. You seem to be making quite a name for yourself, Rookie." He picked up the cigar, which he inhaled between mouthfuls of chicken, and blew smoke across the table. "I've got plans for you, Rookie. But I don't want you getting too cocky. Understand?"

An anxious landlord appeared and asked if they needed anything. One of the henchmen said: "More lush." The landlord produced more stolen hock.

"What sort of plans?" Blackstone asked. He spoke casually, sensing that the answers to a lot of questions were close.

"Steady now," Petro said. "We mustn't rush things. You see I'm a bit bothered about you, Rookie. I don't like people pushing me."

"I'm not pushing you."

"No, but you might. I wouldn't like that, Rookie." He cracked a bone with his teeth and sucked out the marrow. "I wouldn't like that at all."

Blackstone waited, sipping his hock.

"There's a lot happening at the moment," Petro said. "Isn't there, Pascoe?"

Pascoe said there was.

Petro pushed his plate aside and tossed some bones to the Staffordshire bull terrier sitting beside him. He stuck his thumbs in the pockets of his bright waistcoat and said: "I presume you wouldn't mind a little extra blunt?"

"It always comes in useful."

"More than a little, as a matter of fact. By our standards, that is." He belched. "There's a big job coming off, Rookie. I need another man."

"Here I am," Blackstone said.

"It's not as simple as that. I don't know if you're the right man."

"What sort of a job is it?"

"Ah, my covey, that's the point. That's just the point. That would be telling, wouldn't it."

Blackstone poured himself some more hock. "I can't do much if I don't know what the job is."

"True," Petro said. "Very true. What did you say you were inside for?"

"Thieving," Blackstone said.

Petro wasn't impressed. "Not very ambitious."

Pascoe said: "I should have thought Rookie would have been much more ambitious than that."

Blackstone turned on him; Pascoe twisted at his nose. Blackstone said: "You mean like cheating your employers *and* the poor bloody navvies? I don't like that sort of ambition, Pascoe."

Petro said: "I saw that the navvies got their share the other day, didn't I, Pascoe. You see, I have to keep their trust," he explained to Blackstone. "If they thought I was working with Pascoe they might turn on me."

Blackstone filed the information. It seemed as if he had been handed a weapon.

Petro heard his thoughts. "Don't get any ideas, culley. They'd believe me before they'd believe you."

Blackstone thought: unless I got proof. But there wasn't much time. "The job," he said, "what is it?"

"I can't tell you yet," Petro said.

"When?"

"Soon. Very soon. I just wanted to see if you were willing. Me and the boys, that is."

"What sort of a job?"

"It's different, Rookie. Very different. That's all I can tell you at the moment." He pulled on his cigar and blew jets of smoke through his nostrils.

"I don't like mysteries," Blackstone said.

"But you're a bit of a mystery yourself, Rookie." Petro stubbed out the cigar. "Usually," he went on, "I have some sort of test for a new recruit. With those boys it was a spot of wrestling." He indicated the bodyguards. "Who won, lads?"

"Petro did," they said, one after the other. They reminded Blackstone of huge, grotesque dolls.

"There wasn't much point with Pascoe." He grinned. "The only thing he's any good at is cheating and he'd beat the lot of us at that." He stared at Blackstone. "What sort of test could we have, Rookie?"

Blackstone shrugged. "Anything you like."

"Sure of yourself, aren't you."

"Fairly," Blackstone said.

"I think the test should be something different with you because you're a different sort of cove." He patted the terrier's scarred head. "What about some sort of test of willpower?"

"If you like."

"You're a soft sort of cove in some ways, aren't you, Rookie?"

"I wasn't aware of it."

"Oh yes you are. I can tell. I'm quite a judge of character. I don't think you'd do any harm to kids, for instance."

"Not if I could help it."

"Or animals. I shouldn't think you're one for bear-baiting. Or cock-fighting. Or ratting."

Blackstone didn't reply.

"I can tell, you know," Petro went on. "I can tell by the way you treat that dog of yours." He leaned forward. "So this is what we'll do, culley. We'll match our two dogs."

Blackstone clenched his fists. Unfamiliar emotions assailed him. "I thought you said it was going to be a test of wills."

"It is in a way, isn't it? Your will. ..."

"Your dog would kill mine in seconds."

Petro said: "Maybe. You can never tell. It wouldn't be the first time a good little 'un has bitten the ears off a good big 'un."

By no stretch of the imagination was Wagger a good little 'un.

Petro said: "So there you are, Rookie. Think it over. You match your dog with mine. Then I'll let you in on the job." With a final crunch the terrier swallowed its last bone.

Blackstone's dog was waiting for him outside the tavern. A little plumper but still a cur, small and snappy, with its chewed-up ears and ready snarl. Not a very prepossessing sacrifice, Blackstone thought.

Chapter Three

Locomotion was drawn by a team of sweating horses along a long, pot-holed road from Newcastle to Heighington Lane and lifted as gently as if she were made of alabaster on to the wrought iron rails patented by John Birkinshaw. Standing on the 4ft 8in gauge in the sunlight, she looked bold, impatient to steam into the future.

Could anything more go wrong? George Stephenson wondered, patting the smokestack. He liked examining the engine from the front because she looked sturdier that way, ready to butt her way through adversity.

It seemed to Stephenson at that moment that Locomotion was the pistons and wheels of his life. If anything went wrong – and a lot had gone wrong recently – then his life was devalued. The dark caverns of his youth down the mines; the long honeymoon with engines; the effort of learning to read and write and making sure that his only child, Robert, mastered what he had missed.

Stephenson ran his hand over Locomotion's angular parts, remembering milestones: the atmospheric pumping engine at the High Pit, Killingworth, which he had cured; his appointment as engine-wright to all the machines in the collieries owned by Grand Allies at £100 a year; the stationary engines he had built like Friar's Goose with its six-foot cylinder and a nine-foot stroke which could draw a thousand gallons of water a minute from fifty fathoms; his safety lamp for miners and the petulance of Sir Humphry Davy who had invented a similar lamp; his first steam locomotive, the Blücher, followed by the Wellington and My Lord with their chain-couplings; his first meeting on 19 April 1821 with the Quaker banker and woollen merchant, Edward Pease, one of the brains behind the S and D; his appointment as engineer on the line at £600 a year and the foundation on 23 June 1823 of the locomotive works of Robert Stephenson and Co. in Newcastle.

Sunlight flashed on Locomotion's metal. What more could go wrong? He remembered the storms which had sent embankments sliding and maiming navvies; the quagmires through which the men had struggled. Now, Robert had sailed to South America to install steam power into South American mines, and would not be at the opening. And he had been made a fool of by Parliament.

Stephenson grimaced as he remembered Alderson's cross-examination at the committee stage of the Liverpool and Manchester Bill.

The bridge over the River Irwell, for instance. They had agreed to leave 16ft 6in headroom for ships; yet the plans revealed only ten feet when the level of the water was normal and only three feet when flooded!

> Alderson: "So, you make a bridge, perhaps fourteen feet high, perhaps twenty feet high, perhaps with three arches and perhaps with one, and then you boldly say that £5,000 is a proper estimate for it?"
> Stephenson: "I think so.... I merely set out the line for other surveyors to follow."
> "Did you not survey the line of the road?"
> "My assistant did."

Phrases from Alderson's summing-up returned, like old wounds opening up. "This is the most absurd scheme that ever entered into the head of man to conceive.... Did ignorance ever arrive at such a pitch as this?... I never knew a person to draw so much upon human credulity as Mr Stephenson has proposed to do in the evidence he has given...."

They had beaten him on details. On legal wiles. Taking advantage of his dialect. But they could only delay progress for just so long. This was the grand scheme, the world scheme. No lawyer could destroy that.

He gazed at Locomotion, already smelling her hot breath and seeing her banner of smoke unfurl. This was the beginning. Locomotion had to succeed.

Stephenson turned to Sir Richard Birnie, the Bow Street magistrate who showed so much interest in steam. He felt an affinity for this bleak-faced Scot, twenty years older than himself: they had both clawed their way to the top.

Stephenson smoothed his greying hair, brushed forward, and said: "Well, Sir Richard, what do you think?"

"Anything I said would be an impertinence," Birnie said. He had just returned from a meeting with Blackstone who had told him about the threat to the railway, so he asked cautiously: "Are there any weak points that could give trouble on the trials?"

"On the engine or on the railway?"

"Either."

Stephenson pointed at Locomotion's wheels. "There could be trouble there. And possibly with the feed pump and connecting rod-bearings."

Birnie nodded. "What about trouble on the route?" He took a sketch from his pocket. Brussleton Banks, Sims Pasture, Stand Alone, Myers Flat, Honeypot Lane, Fighting Cocks....

Stephenson said: "None of the rails have really been tried out."

"But any vulnerable points where damage could be done?"

Stephenson looked at him suspiciously. "What do you mean – damage done?"

Birnie, who didn't want panic caused by dubious information given to Blackstone by some London harlot, hurried on: "What about the bridges? The iron bridge over the River Gaunless or the Skerne?"

"There's nothing wrong with them," Stephenson said. "The iron bridge is as tough as charity and the Skerne Bridge was built by Ignatius Bonomi" – as if Bonomi had built the Bank of England.

"I see." Birnie lit his pipe. "So there are no *particular* places where there could be any…any failures?"

"Not as far as I know. Although," Stephenson added reluctantly, "if you were really looking for trouble I suppose you'd have a look at the ropes hauling the wagons up the inclines at Etherley and Brussleton."

Birnie had another look at the sketch. Before Locomotion took over, the wagons had to be hauled up the Etherley incline by a fixed, hill-top engine, then pulled by horses to the Brussleton slope where another 60hp fixed engine would pull the train to the top. Locomotion would be hitched to the wagons at Shildon Lane End at the bottom of the incline.

Birnie asked: "Why, have you got any doubts about the ropes?"

"Of course I haven't," Stephenson said irritably. "They're all ready in their drums in the engine houses and they're tough." He was becoming tired of this doubting Scot. "I haven't any doubts at all. You asked where anything might go wrong. That's what I'm telling you. They might go wrong anywhere." He added: "But they won't."

They were joined by Sir Joshua Eccleston and two members of the board. The men who had brought the engine by road sat in the sunshine waiting to see it start.

Sir Joshua said: "What's the hold up?" His manner was bluff but authoritative. "Nothing wrong, is there?"

"No," Stephenson snapped. "Nothing wrong."

"Why don't we start her, then?"

"Because we haven't got a flame."

"No flame?" Eccleston glanced at Birnie's unlit pipe. "Couldn't we kindle a light?"

Stephenson said: "We've sent a fellow called Taylor to Aycliffe to get a candle-lantern."

"Surely the future of communications doesn't depend on a candle?"

Stephenson turned his back and said to Birnie: "Any lead on the highwayman?"

"None," Birnie said. He didn't elaborate for the benefit of laymen.

"And you've had a murder, haven't you?"

"And a riot," Birnie said.

Eccleston said: "I don't think we need worry any more. The robbery seems to have been an isolated incident."

"I seem to remember," Birnie said carefully, "that you had received information about a conspiracy among the navvies. From a man called Frying Pan Charlie, I believe."

"But nothing further's happened."

"Except that Frying Pan Charlie's been killed."

"A brawl," Eccleston said. "You know how the dangerous classes behave."

"What do you think, Mr Stephenson?" Birnie asked. "After all, it was you who called us in."

"We must take every precaution," Stephenson said. He sniffed. "What the devil's that?"

One of the workmen had picked up a wad of oakum and was concentrating the sun's rays on it with the burning glass he used to light his pipe. Smoke drifted from the oakum, then a flame. The labourer pushed the oakum into the fire door of Locomotion; blue smoke wandered from the chimney.

Eccleston said: "What's your name?"

"Robert Metcalf," the labourer said.

When the wheels of Locomotion moved Birnie took Metcalf's arm. "You realize you've made history?"

"Aye," Metcalf said doubtfully.

"That's the first steam locomotive in the world to turn its wheels on a public railway and you started it with a piece of glass and a wad of oakum."

"Aye," Metcalf said.

"Symbolic, isn't it?" Birnie said to Stephenson.

"I suppose so," Stephenson said. Wondering if that was the sort of symbolism he needed.

They met again near the Fighting Cocks. There were handfuls of seagulls on the dry countryside – said to be a warning of bad weather if they came inland. But the warmth and the depth of the sky contradicted them.

Blackstone wore his navvies' clothes and felt at a disadvantage. Birnie was in black which was no surprise. They walked along a lane hedged with tired flowers. A hawk floated high above looking for prey.

Birnie said: "Well?"

Blackstone, who thought that Birnie should be contributing something from his own investigations, said: "How did you get on with Stephenson, sir?"

"A great man," Birnie said.

"I know," Blackstone said. He wished the hawk would swoop and carry Birnie off in its talons.

"We discussed the weakest points on the railway and on the locomotive," Birnie continued. "There seem to be several." He took a cut at the hedgerow with his cane. "Are you really sure they're going to try and wreck it?"

"I'm not sure about anything."

"After all, your informant is only a girl of the lowest class."

Blackstone pushed his cap on the back of his head. "The poorest class," he said.

"She's a harlot, isn't she? A whore?"

"No," Blackstone said, "she isn't." Anger stirred. He walked ahead.

"She lives with a navvy."

"A navvy king."

"Stop being facetious. She consorts with the dangerous classes."

"And that makes her a whore?"

"Very well, have it your way. But she doesn't sound like a particularly reliable witness. What's more," Birnie said slowly, "your judgement seems confused in her case." He glanced at the hawk. "You mustn't let personal feelings influence you, Blackstone."

The hobnail boots felt like lead on Blackstone's feet; the anger was tightening his chest. "If I have any feelings, sir, they're only feelings of pity. The fact remains that she has laid information on which we should act."

Birnie said: "I'm not denying that. I'm merely trying to ascertain the strength of your information."

"Weak," Blackstone told him.

"What about this alleged conspiracy?"

"There certainly was one. That's why Frying Pan was killed. Incidentally," Blackstone said, "the local constable has been unable to find out his real name or address."

"So his gravestone will merely read Frying Pan...."

"No, sir," Blackstone said. "The dangerous classes don't run to gravestones."

"You're being particularly awkward this morning, Blackstone."

"I'm tired of navvying," Blackstone said. He tried to divert his anger. "Have you managed to discover anything at Sir Geoffrey Hawkins's?"

Birnie shook his head. "He's got some of his cronies over there at the moment. They'd do anything to jeopardize the railway." He paused. "Shall we sit down?" Before Blackstone could reply he sat on a log under a chestnut tree. "You know, in a way, you can see their point." He waved his cane, embracing the countryside. "There soon won't be much of this left." He gazed towards the collieries where men had found black gold beneath the grass.

"There's a lot of countryside," Blackstone said. "And there are a lot of men without jobs. The railways will bring them work." But they were wandering. "Perhaps one of your host's cronies might let something slip over the port?"

"Perhaps. But I doubt it. They're fanatics but not fools." He brightened. "Have you ever done any archery, Blackstone?"

"No," Blackstone said. "Not in the Rookery."

"A pity," Birnie said. Blackstone wondered if he was becoming senile.

Blackstone squashed a chestnut, like a small green hedgehog, with his boot; but the nut was yellow and withered. "So where are the wreckers most likely to strike?" he asked. "What does Stephenson think?"

"The inclines," Birnie said. "Brussleton and Etherley. And the engine, of course."

Blackstone nodded. "If someone interfered with the winding gear on the inclines.... On the other hand, they're the most obvious places."

"And these criminals are not obvious, are they, Blackstone? Your friend Challoner is far from obvious. Have you discovered anything about him?"

Blackstone said he hadn't.

Birnie looked at him suspiciously. "I don't want personalities to come into this. I don't want you to settle old scores by yourself."

Blackstone avoided lying by saying: "At least Challoner's presence indicates that there's more to this than merely a tallywoman's gossip."

"Not necessarily. Even if the highwayman *was* Challoner it doesn't follow that he's involved in any plan to wreck the railway. It could have just been a highly profitable robbery. I wondered why he didn't try it again though." Birnie mused. He added: "Anyway, there isn't much time left whatever they plan to do."

"No, sir."

"So what do you propose to do?"

Blackstone smiled. "I await your instructions, sir."

"You usually work quicker than this."

"Short of arresting Petro and interrogating him...."

"You mean beating him up?"

"Short of interrogating him," Blackstone continued, "there's not much I can do except wait for him to recruit me into the conspiracy. And in any case I don't think Petro would break under interrogation – of any sort."

Birnie said: "Then why hasn't he recruited you yet?"

It was like trying to lie to a priest in the death cell.

Intuitively, Birnie seemed to know that Petro had made an approach. "Petro has said he wants me to help him."

"Then why aren't you?"

"First we have to have a trial. A test of strength. He always does that. The idea is that you have to lose."

"Then lose," Birnie said. "Dammit, man, lose."

"Yes, sir," Blackstone said because Birnie wouldn't understand about a small dog with a tail that never wagged.

The hawk fell from the sky, grabbed some small prey, and soared away.

When Blackstone got back to The Rectory most of the occupants were lying on their bunks reading the latest issue of *The Navigator*. It was crammed with death, reproach and warning. Blackstone decided to read it later.

Yankee Tom was on his bunk chewing. He spat into his biscuit tin and asked: "Where are you going, Rookie, when it's all over?"

Blackstone grinned. "Hit the frog and toad," he said, sitting beside the long-limbed American.

"The road?"

"The road," Blackstone confirmed. "Buy myself a new pair of daisy roots."

"Boots?"

Blackstone nodded. "And you?"

"Take a trip on the bright and shiny."

"Briny?"

Yankee Tom nodded.

"You made that one up."

"Sure I did," the American said. "Want to buy my Lord Lovel? My navvy's prayer book?"

"I don't want your shovel," Blackstone said.

"I've been thinking," Yankee Tom said. He sank his teeth into a fresh wad of tobacco. "Why don't you come with me?"

Blackstone sensed the honour: men like Yankee Tom travelled alone. "Are you going back to America?"

"It's about time, I guess."

Blackstone saw the prow of a tall ship cutting through the ocean. Smelled the salt air; saw the coast of the New World on the skyline. Perhaps he could persuade Birnie to let him follow the cheque forger to New York. A working holiday. "I wouldn't mind," he said after a while.

"It's up to you," Yankee Tom said. "Fancy some lightning?"

"I'll take a drop."

Yankee Tom explained that the gin was already watered. He had taken a stone bottle to Pascoe and asked him to pour in two pints. He had then refused to pay the price and refilled Pascoe's two-pint measure. "But I'd already put two pints of water in my bottle," the American explained. "Clever, huh? Both Pascoe and me got two pints of gin and water."

Blackstone leaned back against the wall thinking about Pascoe. If the navvies knew that Petro and he were working together to swindle them they'd cut Petro's throat. If he could prove it he could blackmail Petro into giving him details of the plot. Blackmail him into leading him to Challoner.

Pascoe was the weak link. A signed statement implicating Petro made at gun-point. He decided to see Pascoe later that evening.

"Thanks for the gin," Blackstone said.

Yankee Tom raised his hand.

Blackstone fetched his supper from Alice, creaking away beside her baited strings. On the other side of her sausages spluttered in deep black fat.

He took his chunk of steaming ham outside and fed some of it to the dog chained to a stake. Could he feed him to Petro's killer? He treated the dog with unusual affection, receiving no response.

Man and dog ate their dinner while, beside them, navvies with gypsy blood roasted hedgehogs in the embers of a fire, peeling the spiked pelts cleanly from the flesh.

Blackstone propped himself on one elbow and scanned *The Navigator*. Parts of it were as good as *Hue and Cry*. A navvy wanted "for laying about him with an artificial limb and inflicting grievous harm on several of his colleagues". A warning against a pedlar selling cough mixture which was so strong in its content that "if taken immoderately, it might curtail the patient's life far more speedily than the original ailment". The author, with uncharacteristic flippancy, had added: "Coffin instead of coughing?"

It was not until Blackstone had finished the sermon condemning liquor, brawling and womanizing that he noticed that the letter *t* in *Navigator* was chipped in such a way that it resembled a crucifix.

CHAPTER FOUR

The time had come. Sitting in front of a mirror brushing her hair, Josephine Courtney shivered. She tensed her muscles to control herself, but when she relaxed the shivering began again. With a shaking hand she brushed out the long ringlets, then swept the shining blonde hair back and pinned it severely. Her breasts pushing at her bodice were firm with pouting nipples, but the face staring at her from the mirror was boyish.

She slipped off her petticoats and stood naked, seeing herself as a man might see her. For a moment the shivering was quietened, replaced by a warmth in her loins. Her sister's body was the same – made for love and for children. But her sister never would love now, never be loved. Josephine Courtney began to shiver again.

She dressed carefully in her best green silk and used a lot of perfume. Then she wandered round the room looking for more distractions to delay her. In the corner stood a pile of papers smelling of printer's ink. At the top and bottom were copies of *The Navigator*. In between were hundreds of handbills inciting the farm workers to rise against the railwaymen.

She glanced at a copy of *The Navigator*. Her parents would have been proud of her, distributing God's word among savages – because that's what navvies were. And her sister would have been proud of her; except that these days her sister had no interest in anything, hiding in her room, whimpering whenever she heard a man's voice.

Loneliness assailed her. The loneliness iced with fear that is an uninvited guest on frosty winter evenings; the loneliness of arrival among alien people. She longed for the fireside after tea; for candle-light glinting on copper; for a hearthrug dog; for sewing and reading novels. She longed for the family that had been broken by Petro, king of the navvies.

Their cottage stood on the edge of Sir Geoffrey Hawkins's estate. Her father farmed in a small way. With the little money he earned, supplemented by farm produce, the womenfolk had a comfortable life. Josephine, her mother and her sister, Mary, aged sixteen. Especially in the evenings: that was their time, with the cruelty locked outside and the heavy velvet curtains drawn. On Sundays her father read the Bible aloud while her mother's knitting-needles clicked.

Later, in their bedroom, with its scent of dried lavender, its watercolours and ancient furniture, the two girls lay in the four-poster bed talking until the candle wavered, hissed and died. They talked a lot about romance; about courtship with officers of the Dragoons; although each knew that the best military conquest they could hope for was a soldier – a touch of "scarlet fever". When they had finished with fantasy they returned, almost with relief, to the village boys, to their own kind whom they would choose, court, marry and obey when it suited them. It was all as predictable as the seasons.

They didn't discuss sex; but, living on a farm, they were close to it. Lying in bed, hands clenched between her thighs, Josephine Craig – for that was her real name – often experienced emotions which she could never share with her sister. She knew she should be ashamed of these feelings, but she wasn't.

They heard about the new railway to the north and the navvies who were digging it. Wild, lusty men with whom many girls threw in their lot; but only these sort of girls. Their father warned them that, if ever the navvies came their way, they should stay indoors, lock the doors if necessary.

One night when the flame of the candle was beginning to beat its wings, Mary said: "I wonder what they're really like."

"Who?" Josephine asked. Spring was budding and a young carpenter with prospects had asked her to walk out with him.

"The navigators. They say no girl's safe when they're around. They must be very strong," she added, "with all that work they do."

"Strong," Josephine said, "and wild. Especially when they've taken drink. You stay clear of them." But she was sure the navvies laughed a lot as they caroused beneath the stars; and there wasn't too much laughter in the cottage crouching beside the beech wood.

Mary said: "It must be a wonderful life roaming the countryside. Cooking over an open fire in the fields...."

Josephine knew that her sister saw herself lying in the arms of a handsome navigator with a deep chest and black hair. A romantic, chivalrous navigator. Josephine knew this because her sister was only just sixteen.

"You've been reading too many novels," Josephine told her. "Try reading about the exploits of the navvies in the newspapers."

"They can't be as bad as that," Mary said. "No one could be that bad. According to one report they sell their wives. Surely you don't believe that, Jo."

"No, I don't, because I doubt if they ever get married." A muscular navigator was beginning to intrude into her own thoughts, so she turned on her side in the big, wheezing bed and told her sister to go to sleep. The candle closed its wings and the room was dark, filled with their breathing.

Next day the navigators came. Only three of them, a foraging party from Bishop Auckland way. A navvy named Petro and two hulking companions. Because there were only three the village turned out to have a look, the village boys bold in their numbers.

The man named Petro flashed a lot of smiles around. He wore one gold ear-ring and his hair was black with metallic lights in it, like the hair of the navigator who had visited Josephine and Mary's thoughts the night before.

"He's very handsome," Mary said.

"Too old for you," Josephine said. "Too old by far. I don't like the look of him," she added.

The three banditti went to the village inn, the Jolly Farmer, and drank the best brandy chased by tankards of ale.

The village boys grinned from the doorway before venturing inside. When the three navvies failed to react they began to cheek them as though a wager were at stake.

Petro held up his hand and everyone was quiet. "What are you scared of?" he asked. "There's three of us and a score of you."

Someone at the back of the group said no one was scared.

"Who said that?"

No one answered.

"And you're not scared?"

The same voice answered. "I'm not scared." It was Josephine's carpenter.

"Come here boy," the navvy called Petro said.

The carpenter, twenty years old, stepped forward.

"What's your name?" Petro asked.

"It's none of your business."

"Why do you treat us like this?"

"Because we know what you are."

Petro appealed to the rest of the villagers. "So he knows what we are. Shall I tell you what we are? We're workers like yourself trying to earn an honest living. And I'll tell you something else." His voice had a magnetic quality. "We're working to bring a new prosperity to this land of yours. When we've finished this railway there'll be more brass around than you've ever dreamed of. Instead of slag heaps" – he pointed north – "you'll have heaps of gold. Sovereigns, yellow boys." He wiped the sweat from his forehead. "So why jeer at us? – three fellow workers who've come to make an honest living and bring you wealth."

Feeling wavered. But what about the countryside? What about the cinders? Unemployment? Cows running dry?

"What do you want with us?" the carpenter asked.

Petro appraised him. "First," he cried, "your company." To the dubious landlord he said: "Drinks all round."

Petro had won.

When their tankards were foaming, Petro said to the carpenter: "I'll tell you what we want – we want girls."

The carpenter started to reply but someone else shouted: "How many do you want? We've got plenty."

Petro grinned. "Just three," he said. "We're not greedy."

The carpenter thrust his way out of the crowd and found Josephine outside. He tried to re-assert himself but it was hopeless. Josephine's attitude was maternal. They walked to the end of the main street and back. When she got back Petro had gone; so had Mary.

The next time she saw Mary, four hours later, she was bleeding and sobbing, with her dress torn, one eye swelling, blood spotting her shoes, romance and courtship and love torn from her for ever.

Petro had made his approach to Josephine Courtney, the missionary, the day before. As, somehow, she had always known he would. He had treated her differently to other women and she wouldn't be surprised if he asked her to marry him, to become his queen. Because she was literate, because she was different, because she was holy and untouchable.

She thought Petro would derive a peculiar satisfaction from making love to a woman such as herself: it would be more than a sexual act – it would be a defilement. Josephine Craig was surprised at her instinctive knowledge.

He had come to her lodgings offering to distribute *The Navigator*. Two of his thugs waited outside in the road; she was pleased that Rookie wasn't one of them. Her instincts were alert to him, too. If he wasn't a highwayman then he was a highwayman's twin. She didn't object to highwaymen except when they killed; highwaymen had once figured, remotely, in her discussions about romance with her sister. The moonlight and the mask and the legends of chivalry.

She welcomed Petro with enthusiasm. She was supposed to want his support and that was the way she had to play it. But was it possible to disguise hatred when it was as intense as hers?

Petro was polite. He was scrubbed clean, his hair was freshly oiled and his breath smelled of peppermint. He was also nervous, one hand feeling for the missing lobe of his ear. She offered him tea.

"Thank you, ma'am. You're most kind." He sounded like an actor rehearsing his part.

"To what do I owe this pleasure?" she asked, wondering whether she should sink the knife into his back or chest.

"I thought you might like some help. A larger congregation, perhaps?"

She looked a little coy. "That would be very pleasing. I had hoped more of your men" – she was pleased with the *your* – "would attend my services of their own accord. However, I don't think God would mind if they were *led* to his presence."

"No, ma'am."

The landlady brought the tea. She had objected to having a navvy on her premises, but a florin had banished her objections.

Petro held his cup awkwardly. He said: "I could round them up next Sunday if you like."

She smiled gratefully. "That would be very agreeable. Once they've listened they'll come again."

"They'll come again," Petro said. "You needn't worry about that." His nervousness was evaporating. "No fear at all." He sucked his tea noisily. "We'll be moving on soon. I suppose you know that."

"I presumed so," she said, "because your work is finished here. Where will you be going?"

"It all depends," Petro told her. "There'll always be work for navvies. I reckon we'll start digging this new railway between Manchester and Liverpool. If it ever comes to anything. It all depends on the S and D."

"But that's finished," she said in surprise. "Isn't it?"

"Finished," he said. "But not started. If you see what I mean."

"Not really," she said.

"If anything goes wrong before the opening then they might put paid to the Manchester railway."

Josephine glanced at the anti-railway handbills concealed between *Navigators*. She arranged their distribution but this was of secondary importance to her main preoccupation, which was killing Petro.

She said: "Do you think something may happen?"

"Anything's possible," Petro said.

She poured him some more tea. "You may smoke if you wish."

"It wouldn't be right in your room," Petro said. He picked up a copy of *The Navigator*. "I could help you sell this, too."

"I don't *sell* God's word."

"Why not? You could build a little church or something."

"My work lies with the navvies." She found it easier to lie this way, thinking something and saying the opposite with the forcefulness of your thoughts. "I can't stay in one place."

"We're very honoured," Petro said, "that you should have come among us." He became bored with the cup and poured some tea in his saucer. "Why did you choose us? There are many other worthy causes."

"Everyone seems to be against you," she said. "Even some of the clergy. They don't even want navigators in their churches."

"It's because we belong to the dangerous classes."

"I think you're just misunderstood."

Petro looked doubtful. "Anyway," he said, "I think we should charge a small amount for distributing *The Navigator*."

"But the men can't afford it."

"They'll afford it. And they'll pay – I'll see to that."

"Very well. If you don't think the men will mind. How much should we charge?"

"A penny," he said. "I'll get my special lads to see to it." He paused. "Rookie's a good man. I hear you've seen him once or twice."

"Once or twice," she said warily.

"There's something about him...."

"He's had a hard life," Josephine Craig said.

"He's had that all right," Petro agreed. "Haven't we all?" He stood up and some of the nervousness returned. "I admire you, Miss Courtney."

"Thank you," she said.

He put out his hand as if to touch her. Disgust spurted like warm acid inside her. She backed away.

Realizing that she couldn't be too remote, she managed a frozen smile. "We must have another chat about *The Navigator* and the services."

He snapped at it like a hungry shark. "I'm glad you said that."

She waited.

"I was thinking. Perhaps you'd like to come over to the cottage tomorrow night? We could have a meal and some wine. You do drink a glass of wine?" he asked anxiously.

"Oh yes," she said, "I quite like wine." I mustn't seem too eager, she thought. "But I don't know whether I should...."

"My men will be outside."

The last thing she wanted was anyone outside. "I should prefer it if we were alone." She listened to herself speaking, amazed.

Petro grinned. "If that's the way you want it." His hand came out again. She moved to the door, saying, "I have an appointment."

Petro shrugged, victory a formality now. "Until tomorrow then."

She nodded. "Until tomorrow."

And now it was tomorrow.

She picked up the knife and examined it, drawing one finger down its blade, wondering how much force was necessary to thrust it through a man's ribs.

She was sick with what she had to do and she thought she might vomit. She steadied herself by thinking of her sister, her beautiful sister, whimpering in her bedroom. She steadied herself by remembering the grief and incomprehension of her parents. She steadied herself by recalling the inability of the law to do anything; the constable had seemed scared of the navigators and one had implied that her sister must have been willing.

She put the knife in her bag, took a last look around her sanctuary, opened the door and walked down the stairs into the street.

Blackstone said: "Good evening, Miss Courtney."

She started to tremble again. "Good evening, Mr Rookie. A fine evening."

"You're shivering," he said.

"I'm a little cold."

"On such a fine evening?"

Inventiveness failed her; she tried to smile but failed.

Blackstone said: "Where are you off to on such a fine evening all by yourself?" He peered at her. "And dressed to kill, I see."

She started, words trapped in her throat.

Blackstone smiled. "Just a phrase. Not to be taken literally."

"What are you doing here?"

"I was merely paying you a call. But as you're going out I'll walk with you."

"No," she said.

"You shouldn't be out alone in the streets."

"I can take care of myself. Now, please, I must go. I'm late already."

"For what? A service?"

"Yes," she said gratefully. "A service."

"Evensong? And without a Bible?"

"There's one at the church."

"Which church?"

She was becoming desperate within the labyrinths of untruth. "The village church."

"It's closed for alterations," Blackstone said.

"Is it? How absurd. They didn't tell me."

"So you won't be going anywhere this evening."

"I must," she said. She wasn't sure what she was saying any more.

"Must?"

"You don't understand."

"I understand a little," he said. "For instance I understand that you're a prater."

"A prater?"

"Someone who impersonates a preacher."

"How dare you!" It sounded so weak. "Now please let me go."

"I feel we should have a chat. Especially as you've got nowhere to go, Miss Courtney. If that's your name," he added.

"I don't know what you're talking about."

"I think you do." He took her gently by the arm and was surprised by the violence of her reaction. She tore herself free and, as she did so, her bag flew open and the knife fell on the cobblestones.

❧ ❧ ❧

It took half an hour for it all to come out.

"Was I such a bad missionary?" she asked him.

He told her that she was good; but she should get her Biblical quotations correct and not use the same typeface for both inflammatory handbills and religious exhortations. He also told her not to kill Petro.

She was quiet and the trembling had stopped. They sat at the bow-window watching evening gathering in the village. Blackstone imagined it at Christmas with cherry-nosed children singing carols and the snow that fell during sleep sparkling and undisturbed next morning.

"You haven't answered me," he said.

"I came to kill him. My sister must be revenged." She lit candles and sat down again, the impetus of the evening destroyed. "After all, it's what the Bible says...."

"An eye for an eye?"

"Eye for eye, tooth for tooth, hand for hand, foot for foot. Exodus," she added.

Blackstone spoke gently. "Think of your mother and father. They've got one daughter scarred by this man. If you kill him then you'll be caught and imprisoned and...." He spared her the gallows. "Can you do that to your parents? Two daughters taken from them because of this man Petro. Besides," he said, "your sister may recover. You can become a family again. You mustn't let Petro win this way."

They stared at the knife lying on the table between them.

Blackstone said: "Could you have gone through with it?"

"Oh yes," she said. "I could have gone through with it."

"But not now?"

"I don't know."

Blackstone took the knife and stuck it in his belt. "You must promise me you won't try."

"You didn't know Mary," she said. "The way she was before he came. All she wanted was a little romance. Then a husband and children. Instead she got Petro." Her voice thickened. "He should die, Rookie. He should die for what he did. So that he can't do it to anyone else."

Blackstone took some snuff. "If I attend to it," he said, "will you promise not to do anything?"

"What could you do?"

"Kill him," Blackstone said abruptly. "Do the hangman's job."

She looked at him wonderingly. "Just who are you?"

"It doesn't matter. Just promise me. Petro's a murderer. I'll look after him."

"You aren't a navvy?"

"It doesn't matter who I am."

"And your brother...."

"I found him," Blackstone said. "Thank you for your help."

She stood up and drew the curtains, separating the two of them from the evening. "All right," she said after a while. "I won't do anything. I'll leave it to you." She paused. "He's waiting for me now."

"That," Blackstone said, "is the least of our worries."

She said: "Thank you, Rookie." Then she was in his arms, crying at first, then kissing him and moving her body against his.

"Oh, God," she cried later. And later still: "I didn't dream it could be like that, Rookie."

"That's the way it should always be," he said.

He dressed and left her, telling her to lock the door. As he walked back to Shanty Town he kept his hand on the knife in his belt.

CHAPTER FIVE

The first trials were due to start next day; time was running out, Blackstone thought as he dressed. The digging was finished and the rest of the men stayed in their bunks. He took a mug of stewed tea from Alice and went outside the hut. The day was his own, his last chance.

One course was clear. He would cancel the trials and win a sort of victory. But that way he wouldn't catch Challoner. He decided to test the weakest link – Pascoe.

He set out for the tommy shop breathing deeply of the bright air which, for the first time, had a smell of frost about it. As he approached he became aware that something was missing. His baton, he thought at first. He looked round. No dog.

Pascoe was preparing food and liquor for the final randy. Cheeses were piled on the trestle table that served as a counter and casks of brandy were stacked against the walls.

Pascoe looked up warily. "Hallo, Rookie," he said. "What can I do for you?"

"A lot." Blackstone wandered around the shop inspecting the goods and said: "You really do sell a lot of tommy rot, don't you, Pascoe?"

"No more than others," Pascoe said. "Why, what's it matter to you?"

Blackstone sniffed at an open keg of brandy. "Watered?"

"Maybe. Lots of folk like water with their brandy."

"But they like a choice."

Pascoe shrugged. "You can have the good stuff, Rookie. After all we're going to work together, aren't we."

"Are we?"

"Of course we are, culley. You know that. Petro told you, didn't he."

"Working together on what?"

"Petro will tell you in his good time."

"When the job's over?"

"I don't follow you," Pascoe said. He walked round the trestle table and started to put chalk marks on the casks. "So's I know which ones I've watered," he explained.

Blackstone had always suspected that eventually he would have to emerge from his cover. Challoner knew that he was here and therefore Petro probably knew. Now was the time. He wished he had his baton.

"I'm not sure what to do about you," Blackstone said.

"What the hell are you talking about?" Pascoe straightened up from the casks, smoothing his larded hair; his nose looked very loose this morning.

"I don't know whether to hand you over to the local constable or take you back to London."

"Have you gone crazy?"

"It's like this," Blackstone said. "The future of this country lies in the railways. Right?"

"So?"

"The building of the canals was always plagued by cheats and frauds like you. So a decision was made in London. A decision to make an example of one man. You, Pascoe, were chosen. Don't you feel honoured?"

"Who are you?"

Blackstone watched him closely. "My name is Blackstone. I'm a Bow Street Runner."

"Edmund Blackstone?"

Blackstone nodded.

Pascoe sat down on a cask, trembling, his features even waxier than usual. Blackstone decided the shock was genuine. Petro hadn't told him – if Petro knew.

"You'd better have some brandy," Blackstone said. "Make sure it's not watered."

Pascoe poured some into a tin mug, gulped and choked. Some colour returned to his face. "How do I know you're Edmund Blackstone?" The brandy circulated courage. "Can you prove it?"

"I can," Blackstone said. "But not now. You'll just have to take my word for it."

"And why should I do that?"

"Because you haven't any option," Blackstone said, wishing for his baton with its little crown of authority. "Because there are only the two of us here."

The brandy grew stronger in Pascoe's veins. "Why should I have been chosen?" He tried a laugh but it wasn't a success.

Blackstone said: "Because in a way, Pascoe, you're a railway pioneer. A pioneering swindler. You see," he lied, "I know the extent of your swindling. It isn't just confined to victualling, is it, Pascoe? You've been cheating the owners as well. In a way you've been cheating the country." Blackstone's inventiveness took wings. "After the S and D there'll be the Manchester railway. Then railways all over Britain. London, Birmingham, Glasgow, Cardiff.... If people like you are allowed to go on providing shoddy materials and defrauding the railway companies then God knows what will happen. So you see," he said, sitting on a cask opposite Pascoe, "an example has to be made."

"You haven't got any proof," Pascoe said.

Blackstone sighed. "That's already an admission, Pascoe. You're not much of a professional, are you?"

Pascoe poured himself more brandy. "You haven't got any proof," he repeated.

"I've got enough proof to take you to a constable now. Then I'll take you to London where you'll appear in front of the Chief Bow Street Magistrate, Sir Richard Birnie, because we want this case in the London newspapers."

"Bluff," Pascoe said, twisting at his nose.

Blackstone stood up. "There's no bluff about the fact that we're sitting here alone together. It's very early in the morning. The work is finished on the railway and there won't be anyone coming this way for a long time. I shall take you to the constable and formally charge you. I don't have to have proof to do that, Pascoe. And the magistrate knows who I am."

Now, Blackstone decided, was the time to experiment with his theories of interrogation. Tough, then gentle; hot, then cold. He said: "I befriended you once, Pascoe. When Petro was getting tough with you."

There were two dabs of red high on Pascoe's cheeks. "The bastard," he said.

"Bastard? He's your arch cove, isn't he Pascoe? Your leader."

"He needn't have treated me like that."

"He says he had to keep the loyalty of the men."

"Not like that he didn't. Not rough like that. I thought he was going to kill me."

"Perhaps he is," Blackstone said, "when the job's finished. He won't want you any more then, Pascoe. Perhaps he'll make a proper job of drowning you then."

Blackstone poured the contractor more brandy. "Care for some snuff?" He handed him the gold Nathaniel Mills box.

"Posh sort of box for a navvy, isn't it?" Pascoe examined the box. "You could have pinched it."

"But I didn't, Pascoe. I was given that by a grateful client." Pascoe sniffed some of the dark powder up his nostrils and sneezed. Blackstone said: "I might be able to help you. I might even decide not to press the charge...."

Pascoe sneezed again. "What are you getting at?"

"If," Blackstone said, "I get a conviction – and I usually do – you could be transported. At the very least you'll get a stretch on the hulks. But transportation is my guess because they want to make an example. Although, of course, there's always the possibility of the gallows, according to what charge is brought. Can you imagine yourself, Pascoe, waiting in the salt box to get your neck stretched? But if you decide to cooperate...."

"What do you want?"

"I want to know all about the plot to wreck the railway." Blackstone took some snuff. "I'm waiting, Pascoe. And I haven't much time."

Blackstone took Pascoe's horse to ride to the village where Molly was hiding. From there he would go to The Naked Man.

As he rode he analysed what Pascoe had told him. The attempt to wreck the train was to be made as near to Stockton as possible, close to a place called Hartburn. How was it going to be done? Pascoe said he didn't know. Who was behind it? Apart from Petro, Pascoe didn't know. The name Challoner meant nothing to him.

"When?" Blackstone asked.

"Tomorrow," Pascoe said. Which corresponded to what Molly had told him.

"I hope you're telling the truth," Blackstone said. "For your own sake. Who killed Frying Pan Charlie?"

"I don't know."

"It has to be Petro, doesn't it. With my pistol *borrowed* from my bunk."

Pascoe looked at him with surprise. "I don't know what you're talking about." He clutched Blackstone's arm. "You won't tell Petro, will you, Mr Blackstone. Don't tell him I've peached. You know what he'll do…"

Blackstone mounted the horse, wishing he had Poacher with him. "I won't tell him," he said, "if your information's good."

He rode the horse hard because there was a lot more to do today. The trials were due to start from Shildon at 9am. Theoretically all he had to do was check the engine and the line at Hartburn and lay an ambush. But every instinct warned Blackstone: it was too simple. There was a missing factor. He worried about it as he rode beside the railway. By the time he reached Urlay Nook the horse was lathered in sweat, so he reined it in and let it drink from the banks of the River Tees. Then he rode into the village where the girl was.

She was sitting in the parlour embroidering a tablecloth with marigolds; beneath her needle they looked like yellow spiders. When he walked in she threw away her handiwork with relief. "Did you get my message?"

"What message?"

"I sent a boy to Shanty Town to tell you to come here urgently."

"I've been away," Blackstone said. Footsteps creaked in the corridor. "Perhaps we should get out of here."

They walked down the village street.

"What did you want to see me for?" he asked.

She was silent.

"Well?"

She spoke carefully. "I thought about what you suggested."

"All I did was to tell you to lie low. Keep out of Petro's way."

She ignored him. There was a small fair in a field at the end of the street with a few stalls and tents. A German travelling band led by a musician in leather shorts playing a squeeze box, a couple of freaks, some wild animals, a prizefighting booth, a fortune-teller, a huckster selling rejuvenative potions and aperients, and a couple of shies.

Some of the stalls were kept by gypsies in velveteen coats glittering with gold and silver buttons, ear-rings, buckled clogs and long, slick hair. Blackstone looked around warily in case any of his old customers were present.

"Well?" he said. "What was it I suggested?"

She clung to his arm. "Let's go into the fair. I love fairs. You don't see many of them in the Rookery. But you know that, don't you, Rookie?"

"I know you're frightened to tell me something."

"They're a bit scared in the village," she said. "With all these gyppos here. They think they'll steal their horses."

"They probably will," Blackstone said. "If the navvies don't steal them first."

"Let's have a go on the shies," she said.

"Then you'll tell me?"

"If you take me to the fortune-teller as well."

"I haven't got much time."

"There's always time for a bit of fun. We don't get much, do we?"

He bought her an armful of livetts. The prizes – coco-nuts, trinkets, sweetmeats – were stuck on top of poles embedded in sacks of sand. She threw the livetts with dramatic inaccuracy. "Now you," she said. With his last livett Blackstone got a coconut; he felt immoderately pleased with himself. "For you," he said.

Madame Rita, the fortune-teller, gazed into her crystal ball with such glazed concentration that Blackstone suspected she was drunk. She dealt with Molly first. "A wedding – your wedding... nine children, one poor mite perishing before it's hardly taken the air... a serious illness from which you'll recover... a long journey south with a stranger... money." Madame Rita stopped and glanced at them, powdered face sly beneath a mauve silk scarf pulled tight across her hair. "A lot of money...."

"The reward," Molly whispered.

"What was that, my dear?"

"Nothing."

"The crystal's gone blank now. It's stopped talking. But with all that money coming" – she was blinking as if she'd just returned to daylight – "I expect your young man would like to know what the future holds for him. Wouldn't you, dearie?"

Blackstone sat opposite her. "You've come a long way... from a different walk of life... from the other side as it were...."

Blackstone interrupted her. "It's the future I want to hear about."

She held up her hand. "Don't speak like that in the presence of the spirits." She concentrated. "You'll be taking a long journey, too... there's a surprise ahead of you... you'll have a lot of children... and then you'll be going across the sea." She stopped. "The crystal's clouded again." She pushed it away.

"I didn't like that bit about crossing the ocean," Molly said. "I liked all the rest."

"What was it I suggested?" He led her to the drinking booth and they sat down with some ale listening to the bouncing German music.

She sipped her beer and her words were neat and self conscious. "You suggested I went with Petro."

Blackstone crashed his tankard on to the wooden table. "I did no such thing."

"I know you denied it. But you meant it just the same. I understand, Rookie." She put her hand on his arm. "If we're to get that reward then we've got to know the details. And the only way to do that was to see Petro again. Don't look so angry."

"Did you...?"

"No," she said, "I didn't."

"What happened?"

"I went back to his cottage."

"When?"

"Last night."

The bandleader squeezed an unrecognizable tune from his box while at a table near them a thimble-rigger set up his thimbles.

"And what happened?" Blackstone heard the roughness in his voice.

"Nothing *happened*."

"Something must have." He ordered some more ale from a waiter.

"He started to boast, the way he always does. I said I was thinking of coming back to him. Just thinking, mind you. He does seem to have taken a real shine to me, Rookie."

"And then?"

"I played along with him a bit. I said I wasn't interested in being a tallywoman all my life even if he was king of the blooming navvies. He said if I came back to him there'd be a lot of brass soon. More than I'd ever dreamed of. I said I'd heard about his plans before. All this talk about wrecking the railway. For a moment I thought I'd gone too far. He stopped and stared at me for a while. I thought he was going to hit me. Then he just asked, very quiet, 'What plans?' " She tapped her fingers to the music. "I told him he'd been on about them before. When he's taken a little too much lush. And he'd taken some last night, thank God. He admitted there were plans and I said, 'Oh yes, what are they?' "

Blackstone leaned across the table. "Did he tell you?"

"I wouldn't have sent for you otherwise."

"What are they?"

"As far as I can make out it's all quite simple. They're going to wreck the railway at a place called Hartburn near Stockton."

"How?"

"Blind me," she exclaimed. "Isn't that enough?"

"Did he tell you?"

"As a matter of fact he did. It seems there's a bend there. They're going to remove some of the track. When the poor old Puffing Billy comes round the bend it will go straight off the track and down the embankment. Then, when everyone's going barmy, they're going to throw the lengths of rail back again. That way it will look like an accident."

Blackstone sat back, thumbs in his waistcoat. "And everyone will blame the railway. Or the engine. Or both. The S and D will be finished before it's started and Parliament will chuck out the Manchester Bill again."

She frowned. "You seem to know a lot about it."

"A bit," he said. "What happened then?"

"Nothing much. Petro asked me to stay. But I said I'd go back and get my things and come back to him when the job was done. He seemed to believe me...."

"And he didn't lay a finger on you?"

"Not even his little one." She finished her ale. "Are you proud of me?"

"You're a good girl," Blackstone told her.

"So now you've got to move quickly if we're going to get that reward. Who will you go and see?"

"The constable first," Blackstone said. "Then I'll ride to Darlington to see the owners."

"Don't tell them everything at once," she advised him. "Play them along a bit. That way you'll get more brass." Her voice became shy. "Then what will you do, Rookie? I mean when you've got the money?"

"Take you back to the Rookery," he said.

"And then?"

"Let's get the money first," he said.

The Naked Man looked incongruous in this long afterthought of summer. It was a tavern built for white winters with its swinging sign beckoning travellers into the warmth.

Blackstone tethered the horse and went inside to see if there were any messages and get to his baton. The landlord was behind the bar chatting to a couple of farmers complaining about the drought; they usually complained about the rain so they were happy with the change.

Blackstone asked if there was any mail. Sir Richard Birnie, who was sitting in front of the unmade fire, said: "Just one packet. From Liverpool, I believe."

Blackstone tried not to look startled. "What brings you here?" The landlord and the farmers looked interested. Birnie pointed outside. "A private matter."

They walked into the courtyard where Blackstone ripped open the envelope.

Birnie said: "I have information for you." He had developed a tick in one eyelid which indicated extreme excitement. He went on: "Last night I overheard a conversation between Sir Geoffrey Hawkins and Lord Darlington."

Blackstone didn't consider himself to be a malicious man. In fact he later regretted it; but at that moment he could only remember all the patronizing comment, all the cynicism, all the criticism, that Birnie had dished out. Most of it justified, some of it not. He was ashamed of it but it was irresistible.

He said: "I suppose they were talking about the plan to rip up the rail at Hartburn."

Birnie looked deflated; the tick stopped in his eyelid.

"I should be grateful," Blackstone said, "if you could arrange to have a good fast horse waiting for me at the turnpike at Hartburn at seven in the morning."

"Very well," Birnie said stiffly. He stabbed his finger at the letter Blackstone was reading from Liverpool. "You have some information there?"

"Nothing important," Blackstone said. It was his biggest lie since the investigation started.

Near the Fighting Cocks Blackstone turned the horse towards Darlington. One more job remained to be done that day. He patted the two holster pistols he had brought from The Naked Man and the baton inside his waistcoat.

On the outskirts of Darlington, on his way back to Shanty Town, Blackstone met Sir Joshua Eccleston. He was tending to his horse in the courtyard of a coaching inn when Eccleston came over. "Aren't you drawing attention to yourself?" he inquired.

Blackstone shrugged. "Aren't navvies allowed within the precincts of taverns?"

Eccleston avoided the question. "It's merely that I don't want unnecessary risks taken."

"Then don't take one by talking to a navvy in public."

Eccleston toyed with the watch-chain girding his plump little belly. He gazed at Blackstone suspiciously. "What were you doing in Darlington anyway?"

"On pleasure bent," Blackstone lied.

"I should have thought pleasure would have been the last of your priorities at a time like this."

Blackstone shook his head. "It's always been top."

"I shall make a point of conveying your attitude to Sir Richard Birnie."

Blackstone grinned. "He already knows it." He mounted his horse and rode out of the courtyard leaving Eccleston in mid-sentence.

As he galloped away he glanced at a church clock. Midday. He was beginning his last twenty-four hours as a member of the dangerous classes.

Chapter Six

It was 4pm when Blackstone got back to Shanty Town. Most of the occupants of The Rectory were away poaching on Lord Darlington's land. Only Yankee Tom, the wife who had now given birth, two tallywomen and Alice remained. Alice was smoking a pipe held firmly between her gums.

Blackstone looked for his dog. Its rope was still attached to a stake outside the hut but the knot forming the collar had been untied. Blackstone whistled; lurchers, whippets, terriers and mongrels twitched their ears, but no Wagger.

Blackstone wandered up and down the railway. No dog. He returned to the hut and drank some sweet, dark-brown tea. He asked Alice if she had seen the dog; but Alice, who saw everything, shook her head.

At five o'clock the poachers returned with squirrels, rabbits and a hare or two over their shoulders. Blackstone asked them about his dog but no one had seen it. They skinned their dinners and roasted them over open fires.

When the feasting began, steaming meat washed down with ale, the Gorger sat beside Blackstone. "Petro was looking for you today," he said.

Blackstone wondered if the Gorger harboured any gratitude for having his life saved; he doubted it. The Gorger stuffed a whole potato into his mouth and belched loudly.

"Do you have to sit here?" Blackstone glanced inside the hut. His baton and holster pistols were hidden under his straw mattress. He lay on his side staring into the fire, looking at the castles and caverns of thick ash. Tomorrow, then, was the day. He hoped he had exhausted his allocation of mistakes.

"... and you missed it," the Gorger was saying.

Blackstone returned from the castles. "Missed what?"

"The dog fight." The Gorger wiped some grease from his unshaven chin. "Not that it was much of a fight. Much too one-sided."

The coldness came from inside, making Blackstone shiver. He turned to face the Gorger who was enjoying himself. He began to describe the fight between Petro's Staffordshire bull terrier and Blackstone's mongrel. No one had even bothered to lay odds, he said. "Although he was a game little bastard," he added.

"Where is he now?"

"How should I know?"

Blackstone walked across the field to Petro's cottage. The two resident bodyguards looked at him without interest because he was almost one of them now. He walked round the side and found the dog's corpse. It was bloody and its head had been savaged; but its tail was undamaged, sticking up like a stick of white chalk.

The coldness melted to be replaced by hatred of a ferocity that Blackstone had never experienced before. There was something wrong with his values: the loss of human life should have affected him more. One day soon, he vowed, staring at the cottage with its yellow door. Why not now? He dug his nails into the palms of his hands. There was a job to be finished. Soon. Not now.

He fetched his shovel and dug a grave for the dog. If

they had stayed together, he wondered, would that tail ever have wagged? His eyes were moist as he filled in the grave.

"So," Petro said, "you weren't here for the fight. Pity."

"I thought it was a challenge," Blackstone said. "I didn't accept."

Petro shrugged. He was sitting on his doorstep taking the evening sunlight. "We took it you would accept. You want to be in on the job, don't you?" He glanced around but there was no one within earshot except the two henchmen.

"You shouldn't have done it, Petro."

"If you'd been around we would have asked you. But you weren't were you, Rookie?" He began to whittle a stick with a knife. "Where were you?"

"I went to see a girl."

It was something Petro understood. "Not our missionary lady, I hope." He stared hard at Blackstone.

"I don't touch missionaries."

The shavings curled easily off the stick of wood. The knife was sharp enough to shave with. Blackstone imagined it in his hand and clenched his fists until the knuckles were white.

Petro said: "Anyway, it was more like a rat than a dog. I don't understand what you saw in it."

Blackstone said: "What's the job?"

Petro held up his hand. "Not so fast, Rookie. Not so fast, lad." A head was emerging under his knife on the wood. "You don't have to know the details yet. No wonder you got pinched and had a spell on the treadmill. You're too...."

"Impetuous?"

"You've got quite a way with words, haven't you, Rookie? Quite a way with words for a gonoph. Because that's what you were, Rookie, weren't you? A common little thief."

Blackstone said: "I can't do a job if I don't know what it is. What's it worth anyway?"

"Twenty-five sovereigns," Petro told him. "And it might lead to other things, matey." He held up the piece of wood; the features were coming along nicely; they could have been Blackstone's. "Are you on?"

Blackstone said: "I must know what it is."

"Are you on?"

"All right, I'm on."

Petro handed him five sovereigns; they looked soft and mellow in the evening light. "Five now, twenty when the job's finished."

Blackstone said: "What do I have to do?"

Petro said: "Be at Hartburn at eight in the morning – that's all you have to know."

Plans One & Two
The Execution

CHAPTER ONE

All his life Jonathan Smiles had lived with horses. Born in a stable, the son of an ostler, he had learned to ride before he could walk. There had been hopes of him becoming a jockey but he had grown too thick and heavy. He was a gingery man with pale eyes and slow ways; his features were almost those of a simpleton, but when he frowned the simplicity took on a pattern of brutality; he only frowned rarely, mostly when horses were being threatened, harmed or deprived. Jonathan Smiles dreamed of horses and smelled of horses. And he was very happy working in Sir Geoffrey Hawkins's stables.

The walls of his bachelor room above the stables were hung with saddles, stirrups, brasses, worn horse-shoes, a bridle-and-bit and coloured prints of aristocratic horses who had won classical races. He had also obtained the pamphlets illustrating the demise of the horse when the travelling steam engines took to the iron roads. When he looked at Old Dobbin and his emaciated friend sadly watching the locomotive snorting past, cinders flying, tears came to Jonathan Smiles's eyes. If only he could do something to help them.

It was Sir Geoffrey Hawkins who told him that he could. Jonathan was astounded, overjoyed. Was he game? Of course he was game if it meant putting Old Dobbin and his friend back into harness, if it meant pushing the iron horse off the rails for ever. Next day Sir Geoffrey brought a tall, forbidding stranger to Jonathan's room, a man with London soot in his voice, harsh lines on his face and a slight limp. Not the sort of man, Jonathan thought, to have much feeling for a nag.

They sat at Jonathan's table while the stranger asked a lot of questions. He seemed to have a lot of authority despite his sharp, uneducated voice because Sir Geoffrey, immaculate in riding jacket, jodhpurs and glossy boots, sat back and let him do most of the talking, periodically slapping his boots with his riding crop.

Jonathan couldn't grasp the point of it to start with. There were to be unofficial trials of an engine called Locomotion which were to remain secret in case anything went wrong. Right. Then how did the stranger – whose name Jonathan never caught – and Sir Geoffrey Hawkins know about the trials if they were secret? This, he was told, needn't concern him. Right. Jonathan stuffed tobacco mixed with straw into his pipe and lit it. From time to time he glanced at the loudly-ticking clock on the wall because the horses would shortly be due for their feed.

The stranger caught his glance. "We'll have some more chats," he said. "I can see I haven't got your whole attention. But I'll tell you this much. I want you to have a horse-drawn wagon ready to go on the railway on the morning of the trials."

"Right," Jonathan said. But he worried a lot about it afterwards. What would happen to his horse when confronted with a powerful, hissing monster? Jonathan didn't like it and he determined to tax the stranger with it, convinced that he would have Sir Geoffrey's support if the welfare of one of his horses was at stake.

The next meeting was held in the stables. They housed a dozen horses groomed by Jonathan and one other boy. The boy was absent and the only audience was the horses, recently fed and watered, munching and occasionally kicking the stable-doors without anger.

Sir Geoffrey was again accompanied by the stranger. The stranger continued with the explanation; Jonathan concentrated so that he frowned and looked brutal. There was still a future for horses on the railways if the locomotives could be ridiculed. In fact, said the stranger, Sir Geoffrey, whose views about the S and D were well known, favoured the use of horse-drawn trains on the line. Wasn't that so? Sir Geoffrey said it was and he might even be prepared to put some money into any scheme that precluded steam-engines.

"It's as simple as this," the stranger said. "There's a loop not far past Shildon. It's supposed to be for horse-drawn wagons to get out of the way when a steam engine comes along. But why shouldn't the steam engine get out of the way and let the horse-drawn wagon pass?"

"Why not?" Jonathan agreed. He waited for an explanation.

The stranger said: "So this is what I want you to do, Jonathan." Jonathan could feel that he was trying to be kind. "I want you to be on the line just this side of the loop at 8.45 on the morning of the trials. And I don't want you to give way whatever happens. Locomotion must stop." He was very emphatic. "Then it will have to give way and go on to the loop. Steam gives way to horse. Very undignified." He laughed briefly. "Think you can do it, Jonathan?"

Jonathan frowned. "What about the horse?"

"What about it?"

"It won't get hurt in any way?" He turned to Sir Geoffrey. "It won't, will it?"

"Of course it won't," Sir Geoffrey said. "You have my word for it." Which was good enough for Jonathan.

The stranger took a small bag of sovereigns from his pocket and spilled them on the table. "What's more, Jonathan, there's twenty yellow boys in it for you if you do your job properly." He slid ten across the table. "There – ten now and ten when you've stopped that steam engine." He pointed at Old Dobbin staring hopelessly over the fence. "They'll be back in harness and we'll have horse railways all over Britain if you do your job properly."

"As long as they don't make 'em pull too much," Jonathan said. He picked up a couple of sovereigns and felt their smooth sides. Twenty guineas was more than a year's salary. He weighed the coins in his hand while the two men watched. "I've never seen so much brass," he said.

"Don't spend it too quickly," Sir Geoffrey warned. "Don't draw attention to yourself. And don't tell anyone what's passed between us."

They came twice more, going over the details again and again. Jonathan still couldn't grasp how this one incident on secret trials could affect the future of steam; but repetition soon dulled the queries in his mind.

On the morning of the unofficial trial he was up well before dawn. He fed and watered the horses, wishing, as he had wished every morning for weeks, that it would rain steadily for a few days to give the horses a good green feed of grass before the snows, which he knew would be bitter when they came: they always were after a soft late summer, and the berries were clustered thick and red on the holly bushes.

For the job in hand he was using a cart-horse provided by the stranger. A patient, muscular animal with huge feet that made Jonathan feel sad. The wagon was already on the loop and all he had to do was hitch the cart-horse to it and lead it on to the main line.

He was at least an hour early when he took up his position and he felt hungry. The horse neighed, pawing the ground with its big feet. Jonathan took six pieces of sugar from his pocket. He gave four to the horse and ate two himself.

Much farther down the line Blackstone scouted the area around Hartburn. It was dawn, milky and wet underfoot.

On one side of the embankment stood a line of trees knitted together with thickets. They would be cover for the Irish navvies, outside Petro's influence, recruited to do battle with any wreckers. On the other side stood some coal sheds and a water-tank – the first permanent camp followers of the railway. Soon they would be joined by chimneys sprouting up, mine shafts groping down; by rows of cramped cottages; by riches for the few and poverty that kept you just the right side of starvation for the majority.

Blackstone didn't have time to philosophize. The coal sheds and the water-tank would also provide good cover.

He ran to the turnpike to check the horse. It was no Poacher. A black stallion with a sprinter's muscles and a soft mouth. But no evidence of stamina. Blackstone stroked its neck. The horse had a vital part to play and he hoped stamina was a hidden quality. He was fond of gentle horses, but not today. He gave it some sugar.

Then he returned to the point where the wreckers were supposed to strike. He still wore his navvy's dress; full regalia because it was the last time he would wear it.

Birnie dressed with care. Black trousers strapped under his shoes, black swallow-tail coat, white ruff at the neck. It was going to be an unusual morning so he dressed the way he had dressed for the past twenty years to combat it.

The previous evening had been indulgent, with Hawkins and his landed cronies making too many after-dinner toasts.

"To progress" – from the Earl of Derby.

"To progress," they had agreed, Lord Darlington adding, "However you like to interpret it."

"Surely progress is going forward," Birnie said.

"Not necessarily," Sir Geoffrey Hawkins murmured. "There is a stem of progress. A stem that becomes a trunk. Occasionally there are branches which are superfluous to the true growth." He smiled at Birnie, remembering, Birnie suspected, the fifty guinea bet. "They have to be chopped off."

Birnie said: "Gentlemen, whether you like it or not, steam locomotion is progress. Evolution if you like. Nothing can stop it."

"We shall see," Hawkins said. "In fact I'm quite looking forward to the opening of the S and D. It promises to be quite a banquet at Stockton Town Hall."

"Quite a banquet," Lord Darlington said. "You will be there, Sir Richard?"

Birnie said he would. Try and stop him!

A patronizing smile jumped round the long, candle-lit table; as if they were linking hands beneath it, Birnie thought. He tried to extend the information he had obtained – the information treated so cursorily by Blackstone. He asked: "Is there any reason why I shouldn't?"

Hawkins spoke quickly, trying to forestall the others. No reason at all, he said.

They drank their port and a considerable quantity of brandy. Birnie wished he hadn't drunk so much: he had been trying to keep up with all those titles. Childish. Or so it seemed next morning, before dawn, when he had to get to Hartburn to safeguard progress.

In his black clothes, relieved only by the white ruff, he slipped from Hawkins's fairy castle and walked to the stables with a throbbing head.

Locomotion looked very jaunty this fine morning, standing at the bottom of the Brussleton incline, with ten new wagons loaded with coal, and a thread of smoke coming from her tall smokestack.

George Stephenson and his brother James were present, with William Gowland, the fireman, and Sir Joshua Eccleston. All were sworn to secrecy.

"A great moment," Sir Joshua said. "An historic moment."

"Aye," George Stephenson said.

"If this trial is a success then I feel we should tell the world. We lead where others follow."

"And if it isn't a success?"

The glory on Eccleston's pulpit features clouded. "You don't think there's any chance of failure, do you?"

Stephenson tapped the cast-iron wheels. "I'm a bit worried about those."

Eccleston stared at them, giving them spiritual power. "They'll hold," he said.

"I'm glad you think so." Stephenson, who appreciated Eccleston's money but not his views, climbed on to the wooden platform running along the side of the engine, checked the connecting and eccentric rods and, experimentally, gripped the throttle handle. A dangerous place, the platform, with the rods passing through it, especially if you had to squeeze past two rods – main and eccentric – to reach the valve cross shaft to put the engine into reverse.

Stephenson climbed down to inspect the tender. Half a ton of coal there and 240 gallons of water in its rectangular tank. God knows what the total weight of the train would be on the opening day with more than thirty wagons to haul.

"What speed do you think she'll reach?" Eccleston asked.

"She might make fifteen miles an hour," Stephenson said. "Average about eight."

"Fantastic," Sir Joshua said.

Stephenson looked at him cynically. "Of course it's a very different design from my last engine. The drive from the piston rods to the connecting rods is done with half-beams and parallel motion."

Sir Joshua looked vague. "Revolutionary," he murmured.

"Quite the reverse," Stephenson said.

"Ah."

"The only real advancement is the connection of the wheels by coupling rods instead of chain and sprockets."

"I see that," Sir Joshua said, adding hurriedly: "Shall we get started then?" He sounded as if he were taking Sunday School.

"Aye, we might as well."

"Who's driving it?"

"To start with James and Gowland. I'll take over later."

"Are you taking any passengers?"

"Not this time."

Eccleston took his arm. "I want you to take two," he said. "In the first wagon. Both armed." Before Stephenson could reply he went on: "You see, George" – he usually called him Mr Stephenson – "I've taken a bit of a risk. As you know we've got to get a lot of money to Stockton for the last big pay-out. Contractors, engineers, navvies. I don't trust the stagecoach any more...."

Stephenson said: "Blind me, man, you don't mean all that money's on the train!"

Eccleston's voice acquired a fanatical note. "Don't you see, George, what a great boost it will be for steam locomotion? The owners trusting all that money to the railway. When the money went by road it was taken by a highwayman. When it goes by rail nothing can stop it. What's more, it will reach its destination in half the time. We must show our trust in our own invention, George. This is our chance. I can see it in *The Times* now. Our enemies won't stand a chance. What's more," he added slyly, "anyone with any ideas about stealing the money will presume it's going by stagecoach tomorrow."

Stephenson said: "Have you let the Bow Street Runners know about this?" He thought Eccleston was a bit cracked.

Eccleston shook his head. "I don't trust them."

"If you don't trust them you don't trust anyone."

"Peel doesn't trust them. Nor do a lot of other people. They're too close to the criminals they're supposed to be catching. Not much to choose between them in my opinion. Do you remember the description of the highwayman?"

"A tall man with a limp...."

"And a mask," Eccleston interrupted impatiently. "But, if you think about the full description, it might have been Blackstone. So, you see, I've decided to take the initiative. After all, what has Bow Street achieved so far?"

"There hasn't been another robbery," Stephenson said.

"Because the thieves may be waiting for the big one," Eccleston said. "This man Blackstone hasn't even succeeded in unmasking the conspirators among the navvies. Is it possible that he's working with them?"

"I was quite impressed with him," Stephenson said. "And Birnie is as straight as a die. That's why I called him in."

"Without consulting me," Eccleston said. "Or anyone else for that matter."

"Where's the money now?"

Eccleston led him to the black coach in which he had arrived. Inside sat two men, with hard faces and watchful eyes. Each had two pistols in his belt and a carbine across his knees. In between them were two large black-leather bags.

"There's the money," Eccleston said. "They'll be travelling in the first wagon. I've already seen to it that some of the coal has been removed. They won't mind getting a bit grubby – they're being well paid."

"I think it's madness," Stephenson said.

"You're paid to build railways," Eccleston told him. Seeing the anger on Stephenson's face he added: "Damn good ones, too."

"Thank you," Stephenson said drily.

"So let's get started." He told the two guards to take up their positions in the first wagon. "Now get up steam or whatever it is you do," he said to Stephenson.

James Stephenson, George's elder brother by two years, who had previously driven Blücher, climbed on to the platform with Gowland, the fireman, sitting on the tender.

James Stephenson eased the regulator open, chain couplings clanked taut. Slowly, very slowly, Locomotion's big wheels began to turn. The train inched forward.

In the first wagon the two guards fingered the triggers of their carbines.

Two hundred yards past the loop where Jonathan Smiles stood with his cart-horse and wagon, Henry Challoner waited on horseback in a copse of beech trees. He wore a mask and he had one flintlock, recently converted to percussion, in his hand, another in his belt. He wore a cloak despite the warmth of the morning and the hat with the contemptuous brim. Beside him, also on horseback, was his accomplice, a professional highwayman called Minter, who had helped him with the stagecoach robbery.

They waited patiently for the first puff of smoke on the skyline. There was no one in sight, little movement in the straw-coloured countryside. But neither was relaxed; their hands were tight on their guns, their thighs gripping the horses. You didn't relax when you were about to stage the world's first train robbery.

Challoner touched his companion's arm and pointed. Minter stared across the countryside, eyes glittering in the slits of his black mask. He nodded. The train was coming.

The Irish navvies were hidden behind the thicket on one side of the line and the coal sheds on the other. They were sober because they were getting paid for the job on that condition and because they planned to revenge themselves later for that Scotsman's wedding-day humiliation.

Three constables, two magistrates and Sir Richard Birnie were also present. The local officials asked Birnie why the tall, black-haired navvy known as Rookie had so much authority; Birnie didn't enlighten them.

Watching Birnie sitting on his horse, full of the occasion, Blackstone again felt guilty. Birnie managed to inspire a variety of emotions in him. He had to resurrect the humiliations he had suffered at Birnie's hands to assuage the guilt; it didn't work because nothing could alter the fact that he was using the old man and making a fool of him.

When it was all set up Blackstone fetched the horse from the turnpike, checked the pistols and leapt into the saddle. He wore riding boots beneath his moleskin trousers and his baton was in a holster with one of the pistols. According to his calculations it was time to go.

Birnie said: "Where the hell are you going?"

"Along the line," Blackstone said.

"But the attempt is going to be here."

Blackstone, who knew that no such attempt was going to be made, tried not to lie. On the other hand he didn't tell the truth. He said: "There is something I have to do."

That something was stop a train robbery and take Challoner.

"What?"

"I can't explain now."

Birnie said: "Look here, Blackstone." He glanced round to see if anyone had heard him. "I've never worked with you before. But I've always trusted you even though you failed on one or two of your recent assignments. Now, however, I'm beginning to see why you failed. If you leave here now I can only interpret your action as being one of extreme irresponsibility and act accordingly."

Blackstone said: "Please trust me, sir. You're in control here. Everything will be all right. You've trusted me before, you'll have to trust me again."

"No," Birnie said. The word had a frozen quality about it.

But Blackstone had to be on his way. Already time was running out. "I'll explain later," he shouted. And was gone, leaving Birnie sitting upright on his horse as if he were strapped there.

From Hartburn, Blackstone headed for Elton, Long Newton and Sadberge, keeping parallel with the railway. He calculated that if Locomotion set off on time at 9am Challoner would be waiting about a mile down the track to be out of sight of anyone left at Shildon.

After that it was instinctive guesswork. Blackstone had asked himself: what would I do if I were robbing the train? Whatever he did Challoner would do – or near enough. This, he had decided, is what I would do: take Locomotion at gunpoint and uncouple the wagons. Then force driver and fireman to get up full steam. If Locomotion continued eastwards it would take Challoner and his swag straight to Hartburn where he had been at great pains to stage an extravagant diversion. So what would I do? Blackstone asked himself. He consulted his sketch of the railway. It was obvious. Take the engine along the line towards Myers Flat and Honey Pot and then, instead of continuing along the main line, take the short branch line to Darlington. There, Blackstone thought, I would have a fast horse waiting for me.

Blackstone spurred on the black stallion, taking a route that was never far from the line in case his calculations were wrong. From Sadberge he headed for Great Burdon. And it was in between the two that his horse went lame. Blackstone dismounted and picked up the horse's front right hoof. The iron shoe was a cup of blood. He swore, then patted the horse sympathetically. He should have made allowances for accidents; before the recent failures he would have done so. He looked around – nothing but fields and, in the distance, the black fringes of progress.

Sweat ran down his body under his navvy clothes. A failure this time meant only one thing – a return to the Rookery, a return to the other side of the law. He could either take the horse to Great Burdon and hope there was a smithy there, or tether it to the fence and run there, hoping that someone would lend him another horse.

He smoothed the horse's heaving flanks, tied it to the fence, took his guns and ran down the dusty, pot-holed road. He thought he was in good condition, but soon his heart was thudding: he was used to navvying, not cross-country running.

At Great Burdon, on the River Skerne, he found a stables behind a big, square house covered with ivy. A decent, comfortable house unused to intrusion. He went to the stables because there wasn't time to argue with butlers or footmen.

A groom was saddling a chestnut hunter in the dusty courtyard.

Blackstone said: "I need that horse, lad."

The groom, a boy of about fifteen with a rodent face, said: "You get out of here. We don't want any banditti round here."

Blackstone showed him his baton.

"What do you do with that?" the boy asked. "Play the drums?"

The head groom appeared, a bleak, middle-aged man with bow legs. "What's going on?" he demanded.

Blackstone imagined Challenor leaping on the wooden platform of Locomotion, gun in hand. He saw the engine rattling along the line. He saw Challenor vaulting on to his horse and vanishing with the two black bags.

Blackstone said: "My name's Blackstone. I'm a Bow Street Runner. I must borrow that horse."

"Edmund Blackstone, eh?" The head groom backed towards the stable. "*The* Edmund Blackstone?"

Blackstone said: "The Edmund Blackstone."

"And I'm the Duke of Wellington," the head groom said. "Where did you pinch that baton from?"

Blackstone drew one of the long-barrelled horse pistols, cocked it and waved it from boy to groom. "Give me that horse. One move from either of you and I'll blow your heads off."

"You won't get far," the head groom said.

Blackstone walked slowly towards the chestnut. It was a fine horse, strong enough to carry the stoutest squires. "Get away from it, boy," he said.

The boy backed towards the groom.

Blackstone mounted, whispered to the horse, gave it a touch with his heels and they were away. He glanced behind him: man and boy stood frozen in a tableau. But within seconds they would give the alarm. Blackstone hoped no other horses were saddled.

He thought about galloping across country; it was the sort of ride the big chestnut would have enjoyed. But that way he might miss Locomotion. So he kept to the road running parallel with the railway, Honey Pot then Myers Flat.

He was riding well, the horse looking for a pack of hounds, man and mount moving as one, when he spotted the smoke to his left, moving steadily eastwards.

Locomotion came into sight about half a mile from the loop where Jonathan Smiles waited with his cart-horse. He watched it nervously, wondering about the strength of a ridicule that was witnessed by no one except himself and the men on the engine. Still, he supposed they knew what they were doing. He remembered the feel of the sovereigns and the expression on Old Dobbin's face as he looked over the fence at the travelling engine; an engine just like the one puffing towards him now.

Jonathan Smiles gave the cart-horse a friendly slap on the rump. The horse strained, dragged the wagon forward and stopped on the main line. The engine showed no signs of stopping so Jonathan stood in front of the horse thinking that, if the worse came to the worst, his body would give the animal a little protection.

James Stephenson saw the horse and wagon first. He shouted and rang the brass warning bell. But the driver stayed in front of the horse, arms crossed.

"We'd best shut off the steam," Gowland yelled.

"No time," Stephenson shouted. "Not with this load pushing us from behind."

He edged round the rear main rod pumping up and down from wheel to superstructure. The galloping metal caught his hat and tossed it aside. Wagon, cart-horse and driver loomed nearer.

Stephenson reached the rear-moving eccentric and negotiated its knifing actions. There wasn't time to judge the movement. He grasped the handles of the valve cross shaft and put them into reverse.

Locomotion shuddered. Red hot cinders and smoke belched from her chimney. The iron wheels skidded, showering sparks. Every nut, bolt, piston, rod and valve protested. She careered on, wheels locked.

Within fifty yards of man and cart-horse the backward thrust of the wheels bit. Twenty-five yards. You could feel the strain; but there was Locomotion pushing her wagons backwards, slowly, ponderously.

Gowland shut off the steam while James Stephenson, his face smeared with grease and smuts, jumped down to confront Jonathan Smiles.

"You bloody fool," he shouted. "What the hell do you think you're doing?"

Jonathan, who wasn't sure, smiled, creasing his features into total simplicity.

Stephenson said: "I asked you a question. What do you think you're doing?"

Jonathan patted the cart-horse's nose and said: "Old Dobbin made you stop then."

"Who asked you to stand there with him?" Stephenson asked, conserving his views about Old Dobbin.

"No one," Jonathan said. Sir Geoffrey and the stranger had been very emphatic about that.

"You just thought it would be a good idea?"

"Aye," said Jonathan.

"Why?"

"Someone's got to think of Old Dobbin looking over the fence."

"I'll have you certified," Stephenson said.

"Aye," Jonathan said. He didn't move: he wasn't to move until two men on horseback rode down from the copse.

Stephenson signalled to Gowland. "Come and help me move this idiot."

"Don't you touch me," Jonathan said. "Nor the horse." He frowned, brutalizing his features.

Stephenson and Gowland moved towards him. Jonathan bunched his turnip fists. Down the line, the two masked men broke cover.

Stephenson saw them first. "What the devil!" he exclaimed.

The two men reined their horses and Jonathan led cart-horse and wagon off the main line.

The taller of the two pointed to the wooden platform. "Back up there. Get full steam up. I want 15mph out of her."

"Then you're crazy," Stephenson said. "That means 1¾ revs per second if the whole system. . . ."

The taller of the two men cocked his pistol. "We're going to uncouple the wagons. It'll make it then. Now move." He aimed the pistol.

Gowland said: "I don't know what this is all about but we'd best do as he says." They climbed on to the platform.

In the first wagon one of the two guards took aim and fired. The ball went wide, thudding into a tree. Challoner crouched beside the engine while Minter crept round the back.

Challoner shouted to Stephenson: "Get moving."

He was answered by a whoosh of steam as Locomotion's weight safety valve lifted. The steam shot towards the sky in a fierce jet before scattering into wisps of white cloud.

Challoner leapt on to the platform on the opposite side of the engine to Stephenson and Gowland. "What the hell was that?" He waved his pistol. "Don't try any tricks. This engine has been tested a dozen times." The weight valve clamped down again, cutting off the steam. "If we don't get moving within one minute I'll shoot one of you," Challoner said. "It's as simple as that."

Minter shot at the two guards from behind and they cowered among the coal. He grabbed the two black bags and handed them to Challoner on the platform. They were very heavy.

"Now the couplings," Challoner said.

Minter struggled with the chain, sweat trickling from beneath his mask. It was very peaceful all around; a blue and gold day with a flight of ducks in arrowhead formation heading for the estuary of the Tees. Jonathan Smiles stood protectively in front of the horse: they hadn't told him anything about shooting, but there was another ten sovereigns for him on the condition that he forgot everything he had seen and his memory had never been his strong point.

Challoner peered around. No one behind, no one in front. He imagined Blackstone and his men waiting for the wrecking that would never happen. It was an enjoyable thought. The plan was working perfectly: £10,000 in the two bags, Blackstone making a fool of himself at the diversion which had so carefully been fed to him.

Minter uncoupled the wagon and joined Challoner on the platform. Gowland worked on the tender while Stephenson stood at the regulator.

"I've warned you," Challoner said.

Stephenson said: "You couldn't drive the engine without me."

"Gowland could."

Stephenson eased the regulator open and they began to move backwards.

"Forwards," Challoner shouted. "Forwards, man!"

Again Stephenson negotiated the rods and grasped the handles of the valve cross shaft. Cinders from the chimney ignited a patch of dry grass. Jonathan Smiles stamped out the flames.

Locomotion eased forwards.

Challoner relaxed. He told Minter: "You keep your barker on the fireman. I'll look after our driver." He kept his pistol trained on Stephenson.

The engine gathered speed. Challoner listened to the grind of wheels on rails, watched the rods and pistons accelerating with oiled ease, the banner of smoke streaming behind. He smelled oil and steam and cinders, felt the new power beneath him. If things had turned out differently Henry Challoner might have taken to railways.

There was a clear stretch of rail in front. To Challoner it seemed to stretch to London. To freedom. To wealth. By now they were probably doing ten miles an hour. The stream of air flattened his mask against his face.

Challoner tested the weight of the bags. Gold and notes. With his cut he might settle down; open a tavern or a gunsmith's. The prospects blossomed with the exhilaration of the ride. He might travel, the way Blackstone did, and return to England when his description had been dropped from the *Hue and Cry*.

He noticed Stephenson staring to his left. Challoner followed his gaze. A horseman was riding towards them at great speed. The blossoming prospects withered: the horseman could be only one person.

When Blackstone saw the smoke from Locomotion he cut across the fields, urging on the chestnut hunter; although it needed no encouragement, leaping fences and fallen tree-trunks, expecting its rider to duck under overhanging branches.

Half way to the line he realized that he had underestimated the engine's speed. Like a marksman he should have aimed in front of a moving target. He altered course slightly; it was going to be a race between horse-power and steam-power.

When he reached the track Locomotion was a hundred yards ahead and still accelerating. He wished he was mounted on Poacher, although the chestnut was the best substitute he was likely to find; it was used to chasing a quarry – fox, stag, otter – and didn't mind giving a steam engine a run for its money.

Seventy-five yards. Fifty yards. Horse overtaking steam. But how long could the horse keep it up? Already the veins were standing out on its neck and its breath was snorting.

He could see Challoner's mask. Twenty-five yards. Horse's mane streaming, engine's smoke flying. Challoner raised his arm and aimed his pistol.

Blackstone ducked, clinging low to the horse's neck. But, as Challoner squeezed the trigger, James Stephenson pulled the rope and the bell behind the smokestack rang, making Challoner jerk the twin-barrels of the pistol. The bullet went wide.

Locomotion pulled away again. Seventy-five yards. Smoke and cinders blew into Blackstone's face. He wondered how long the engine could keep it up at that pace; how long the chestnut could.

He urged the horse on. It managed to respond. Blackstone drew one of his pistols, but he was afraid of hitting Stephenson or the fireman.

He was almost level with Locomotion. Within a few yards of Challoner and the other masked man. He shouted at Challoner but his words were whipped away. Challoner shouted back, waving his gun.

Locomotion took a curve, swaying dangerously.

Blackstone heard Stephenson shout: "Slow down... kill us all."

In pantomime he saw Challoner urge him on. Then Stephenson lunged at him but the other masked man who had edged his way to the rear of the engine closed with him.

They fought while the bell rang and the engine continued to pick up speed. The fireman on the tender picked up his shovel but Challoner waved his pistol at him.

High above, another formation of ducks made their lonely, placid way towards the estuary.

The second masked man swung his fist at Stephenson but his heel slipped off the platform. He tried to steady himself, grabbing at the wildly pumping rear main rod; the rod hauled him up and shoved him down again; he cried out with terror, then fell back, pulling Stephenson with him.

Now only Challoner was on the platform. Blackstone grinned fiercely, assessing Challoner's knowledge of driving travelling steam engines. "You'd better jump for it," he shouted.

Challoner ordered the fireman on the tender to take over the controls.

Horse and engine were level but Blackstone could feel the chestnut flagging. He measured the distance from horse to platform. He would have to judge it so that he landed at the back, dodging the leaping main rod.

Challoner took aim and fired. The bullet seared Blackstone's bare forearm. Blood ran down his hand on to the horse's neck.

They were nearing the branch to Darlington. Blackstone steadied himself for the leap. But his arm was weak; and to make the jump he would have to slip his stirrups, sling one leg over the horse's neck and steady himself before leaping; while he did all that the horse would fall behind.

Challoner took another pistol from his pocket. He aimed it but the fireman hurled a chunk of coal at his arm. Challoner swore and turned on him, then realized that, if he shot the fireman, he would have no one to control the engine.

Blackstone took aim. The ball clanged against metalwork. He would have to make the jump. Holding the reins with his left hand, he swung his right leg over the horse's back; but, as he did so, a shower of cinders caught him in the face; he brushed them aside, feeling them burn his cheeks.

Blood streamed down his arm. He steadied himself but the brave chestnut couldn't help any more. Its chest was heaving and they were falling back. Level with the rear wheels, level with the tender. Too late. "Ease up boy," Blackstone whispered. "Ease up."

The chestnut slowed to a canter. Blackstone took a last shot at the masked figure on the platform but it missed. It didn't surprise him.

He reined in the chestnut and dismounted as Locomotion sped away, its smoke a banner of victory.

A mile down the line Challoner ordered the fireman to slow down. He had won but his emotions were mixed: it was always the way when Blackstone was involved. He was never sure whether he had aimed to kill; was never sure whether he was relieved that the process of execution had been interrupted. Why had he delayed so long in the room above the chandler's?

Locomotion slowed to 3mph. Ahead Challoner could see his own horse tethered to a tree. He picked up one of the heavy black bags and tossed it on to the ground, then the other. They made satisfactory metallic thuds as they landed.

Keeping the gun trained on the fireman, he moved to the edge of the platform. "Best go back along the main line to Hartburn, culley," he said. "I hear there's quite a reception committee waiting for you there."

He leapt from the engine, picked up the bags and mounted the horse. Then he was away, heading south to the point where they planned to divide the swag. After that he would ride on south to London.

Blackstone took the chestnut to a nearby stable. He gave the groom a sovereign and asked him to look after the horse until its owner came for it. A chamber-maid noticed his grazed arm and bandaged it for him. Then he set out for Shanty Town. The account wasn't settled yet; among other things he had to see Petro about the dog. He decided to make a point of avoiding Birnie until the opening of the railway. He walked quickly, swinging his good arm briskly. Above him the ducks began their descent towards the estuary.

Chapter Two

The bonfire was twenty feet high and blazing wildly with plumes of sparks and fierce pale flames. It was built from the residences of Shanty Town which were collapsing under the blows of sledgehammers. As the walls fell into the dust the rats made a run for it.

There was a great energy about the men this morning. The job was finished, the wages were due in a couple of days and immediately afterwards the last randy would begin. This would continue for a couple of days more and merge with the celebration laid on by the owners. While guests in evening dress toasted the future of the S and D in Stockton Town Hall the navvies would be drinking gin, whisky and ale in the open and cutting hunks of meat from carcasses roasted whole on spits.

They sang as they piled walls and doors on to the bonfire. Their life was now and they forgot the death and hardship behind and in front of them.

The crones sat in the sunlight while their kitchens collapsed around them. When the next job started they would be there; no one quite knew how. Alice sat in her rocking chair squeezing the last drops of gin from a stone bottle, rocking gently beside her copper pots and her big black frying pan.

Blackstone asked her what her plans were. For the first time that he could remember she spoke more than a monosyllable. He bent to catch the dusty words. "You're no navvy, Rookie. Why should you care?"

Surprise silenced Blackstone for a moment. How many others shared her knowledge? She was speaking again, voice like the rustle of parchment. "Don't worry, culley, I've got the time to watch you all." She beckoned him closer. "You got the muscles all right, but they're all in the wrong places for a navvy."

Blackstone grinned and straightened up. He took a sovereign from his money belt and gave it to her. She looked at him through faded eyes deep in their sockets; he thought one fluttered in a wink but he couldn't be sure.

The air smelled of smoke and decay. Some of the fleeing rats had been caught with nets for sport with the dogs. All the shanties were down now except Petro's. Blackstone stared at its yellow door speculatively.

Yankee Tom cut himself a cud of tobacco and began to chew it. His teeth were quite white despite their perpetual contact with brown dye. They sat on the bald grass and watched two navvies kicking each other's shins.

Yankee Tom said: "Now that it's all over, Rookie, I figure you can tell me what you've been doing. What's your real name?"

How many more? Blackstone wondered.

"Well?"

It didn't matter any more, Blackstone thought.

The American said: "Don't worry about me. I'd just like to know who you are if you come to New York."

"My name's Blackstone."

"Yeah?" He chewed thoughtfully. "On the side of the law, are you?"

"Is it so obvious?"

"Not really. Not to most people. I just happen to be able to spot lawmen. Doesn't worry me. I take as I find.

Who are you after? Him?" He pointed at Petro's inviolate cottage.

"In a way."

"Still mysterious?"

"I've got a score to settle with him."

"About that dog of yours, I guess."

"Partly," Blackstone said.

The foundations of the bonfire shifted and the edifice fell with an explosion of ash and sparks.

Yankee Tom said: "Petro's gone. Taken two of his bodyguards with him."

"I thought as much."

The American frowned. "He could be anywhere by now."

Blackstone stuck out his hand. "I'll be on my way now."

"Will you be at the randy?"

"Maybe."

They shook hands, holding hard for a moment.

"Well," Yankee Tom said, "don't forget about America."

"I won't."

"It's been great," the American said, embracing all the lawless loyalty they had shared. "Have you any idea where you'll find Petro?"

Blackstone spoke abruptly. "I'm afraid so."

Yankee Tom shrugged. It wasn't any of his business. He spat with finality. "Good luck," he said.

Blackstone put his possessions in a sack. He tied this with twine and slung it over his back, the handle of the sturdy, vicious-bladed shovel protruding.

Then he set out for The Naked Man for the last time. He was happy to be through with navvying but he was leaving something behind. He didn't try to analyse what it was.

A mile down the road he stopped and looked back.

Laughter and song drifted towards him and smoke from Shanty Town's funeral pyre twisted into the sky.

He hitched up the sack and strode on. He didn't look back again.

First he bathed in a barrel of steaming water feeling the grease and dirt slide from his body. The wound on his forearm burned, the callouses on his hands softened. His recent life slipped away and dissolved. He dried himself before shaving, using the razor with care because he didn't want any cuts to spoil the transformation. He looked at himself in the long, tarnished mirror to check the different muscles Alice had noticed. But by now he had probably acquired them.

He turned to the clothes which the maid had pressed. Swallow-tail coat, royal blue waistcoat, breeches, long soft boots. New muscles tightened the shoulders of the coat; he would have to take it to Weston for alterations.

Luxury enfolded him. He brushed his hat, straightened his waistcoat and went down the complaining stairs to the parlour.

The landlord almost snapped to attention. Blackstone put his baton on the table beside the unlit fire. He ordered a dog's nose and drank it slowly. He had one more, watching with amusement how hurriedly the landlord mixed the drink. No navvy ever received such attention. He told the landlord to get him a horse.

He didn't drink any more because he needed his wits for what lay ahead. When the horse was ready he paid the landlord all he owed him. Then he went looking for Petro, knowing where to find him and wishing that he didn't.

The first bodyguard, a powerful, stooping man with miner's shoulders, was sitting outside the house where Molly was staying. He gazed at Blackstone in surprise. "Rookie?" he said, "what are you doing here?"

"Not Rookie, Blackstone."

The bodyguard stared at him. "It is Rookie, isn't it? Is this some kind of joke?"

"You mean Petro didn't tell you?" Blackstone dismounted.

"I don't know what you're talking about."

"Well listen carefully," Blackstone said. He took out his baton. "Do you know what that is? I reckon you should with your sort of background."

"Bow Street Runner?"

"Correct. Petro knows who I am. Obviously he didn't want to scare you."

The bodyguard looked baffled. "I don't understand."

"You don't have to." With his free hand Blackstone felt for one of his pocket pistols. "You just do what I tell you and you'll have nothing to worry about."

"Is it Edmund Blackstone?"

"You flatter me." Blackstone watched the man's hands drawing back, tendons standing out on his wrists. "Don't," he warned.

But the bodyguard did. Blackstone kicked his pistol flying. "I could have shot you," he said. "Now throw me the other barker. Very easy," he said as the man's hand went to his belt. "Very slowly. Throw it on the ground in front of you."

The bodyguard tossed the flintlock on the ground. Blackstone picked it up with his left hand, keeping the Manton in his right trained on the man's chest.

Blackstone said: "Now turn round and face the wall." He felt the man's clothes for weapons and found a throwing knife. He held it in the palm of his hand. "Nicely weighted," he said.

The man said: "What are you going to do?"

"I wish I could trust you," Blackstone said.

"You can trust me, Mr Blackstone."

"I can now," Blackstone said, hitting him with the butt of the pocket pistol behind the ear, not too hard. The bodyguard slid down the wall to the ground. Blackstone found some rope in a yard and bound his hands and ankles.

He looked up and down the street. A few dogs, a few children. The village was deep in post-lunch stupor. He wondered about the owner of the house, if his loyalties had been bought.

He tried the door handle. The door was open. He walked into the hall, gun in hand. The silence was thick. He thought he could hear slumberous breathing. A cat ran between his legs. The place smelled of boiled cabbage and roast meat. At the end of the hall was a closed door. Half way down, climbing to the right, was a staircase. The girl slept at the top of the stairs. Blackstone moved towards the stairs trying to disengage his legs from the cat. He stroked it and it meowed. He froze; nothing moved. Elements of the silence asserted themselves – the ticking of a clock, the creaking of woodwork.

Blackstone trod on the first stair. It didn't protest so he guessed the second or third would betray him. It was the third. A creak as loud as the call of an inn sign swinging in the wind. Again he stopped; the house lived around him, breathing and pulsing. He thought he heard a cry above. He started to climb again followed by the cat.

The stairs curved so that he couldn't see the landing. He presumed the second bodyguard was up there. He was, standing at the window gazing down into the courtyard at the back of the house.

Blackstone reached the top of the stairs and whistled softly. The whistle took a moment to register, then the man turned. He was tall with pouchy eyes and a broken nose, a fighter from Birmingham.

He opened his mouth but Blackstone put his finger to his mouth.

"What the hell...." the bodyguard whispered. His puffy eyes narrowed. "It's Rookie, isn't it?"

Blackstone nodded. He crossed the landing in three strides.

The bodyguard's voice hissed. "What are you dressed like that for?"

"Never you mind," Blackstone told him. He pushed the barrel of the pocket pistol in the man's ribs. "One more sound out of you and it will be your last." He stepped back. "Now turn round." He clubbed him and tied him up with the rest of the rope.

From behind the door he heard a cry. The door was frail with a loose handle holding an ancient lock. He stood back and waited till the cat got out of his way.

He hit the door with his right shoulder, holding the gun in his left. It burst open easily, so that he was half way across the bedroom before he could stop.

Petro snapped up. He was dressed in moleskin trousers and white, long-sleeved shirt. The girl was naked on the bed; Blackstone grieved momentarily.

"What the devil...." Petro began. But his reactions were good and he was reaching beside the bed as he spoke. Blackstone kicked the pistol away.

To the girl he said: "Cover yourself up."

She was trembling.

To Petro he said: "Get away from the bed. Stand against the wall."

The girl said: "Rookie, what are you doing here? Why are you all dressed up like that?"

"Don't waste your time," Blackstone said. "No more lies – there's no more point."

"Who are you?"

"You know who I am." A fraction of hope that she didn't know survived. "You must know."

Petro destroyed the hope, enjoying its destruction. "Of course she knows. This is the great Edmund Blackstone."

She was beginning to cry. Blackstone understood. To escape from the hopelessness of the Rookery you would do anything. He had.

She said: "Why have you come here, Rookie?"

Blackstone nodded at Petro standing against the wall. "I have an account to settle with him."

"You're too late," Petro said. Thumb and forefinger searched for the missing lobe of his ear.

"Really? Perhaps you know more than I thought you did." Blackstone crossed the room. "Turn round, hands on the wall." He searched Petro, found a pocket pistol and tossed it across the room. "Now turn round again."

Petro turned. "Very immaculate," he said. "Quite the beau. Out of our class, isn't he duchess," he said to the girl.

She said: "I didn't know at first, Rookie...."

"It doesn't matter."

"What are you going to do now?"

"First," Blackstone said, "a little chat. And then...." He sat down, manipulating his snuffbox with his free hand. "... and then Petro and I will have the test he mentioned once. Not a murder this time, Petro, a fair fight. How does that suit you?"

"Fine," Petro said.

"And if you win you go free. But first the chat." He pointed to a chair. "Sit down there." Petro sat down.

The girl sat up, holding the sheet to her breasts. Blackstone hoped that some of what he was about to say would be disproved.

Blackstone said: "I'm not sure when you first knew who I was."

"Does it matter?" Petro smiled. "Do you mind if I smoke a pipe?"

Blackstone let him smoke, watching carefully as he took the stubby clay pipe and leather pouch from his pocket. Smoke filled the room making the girl cough.

Blackstone said: "It doesn't really matter. But you've certainly known for a long time. Who's paying you, Petro?"

"Go to hell," Petro said.

"Someone must have told you who I was. You're not clever enough to have found out yourself."

Petro sucked at his pipe.

Hopefully, Blackstone said: "Perhaps Molly didn't know when we first met in The Naked Man."

The girl said: "Petro threatened to kill me." She didn't mention their first meeting. "He beat me up. You know that, Rookie...."

Petro took his pipe from his mouth. "Shut your mouth," he snapped.

The girl was silent. Blackstone noticed that the lines of her body under the sheet were still young and firm. But not for long, not this way.

He said: "The idea was for the girl to feed me wrong information. Perhaps" – he nodded the pistol towards Petro – "someone told you I was susceptible to women?"

"Such long words, my dear," Petro said.

"So it was her job to make me believe there was some sort of plan to wreck the railway. She played her part very well," Blackstone said reluctantly. "First the vague suggestion that an attempt was going to be made. Then, on the eve of the trials, she discovers the exact spot. The timing was perfect and I played into your hands when I broke into your cottage and when I went after Pascoe. Pascoe confirmed Hartburn with very little persuasion. The perfect diversion to the robbery was all set up."

Petro puffed complacently at his pipe. "The almost perfect diversion," Blackstone corrected himself.

Petro took his pipe from his mouth, looking worried for the first time.

Blackstone went on: "Because, of course, there had only ever been one plot and that was the theft of the last big pay load. It had two purposes, didn't it, Petro?"

"You're the expert," Petro said.

"Firstly robbery for gain. A lot of blunt involved there. Secondly to incite the navvies into a final fury. I've no doubt you plan to tell them to wreck the railway. An end of the S and D, an end of the Liverpool–Manchester. An end of railways for a year or so. You've prepared them for it quite nicely, haven't you, Petro. The first highway robbery – wages delayed. Then the next pay-day delayed again because I had arranged for the stagecoach to set off two days late to avoid the highwayman. The navvies would go crazy this time – especially if they were told the owners didn't intend to pay them at all." Blackstone took some snuff. "It's all been very clever. Too clever for someone like you."

"You don't imagine I'm going to help you, do you?" Petro said. "I'm not a nose."

"It doesn't matter. Only a man like Challoner could have worked all this out."

The girl said: "I didn't know any of this, Rookie...."

Petro turned on her. "Shut up you little whore."

The cat came in and rubbed itself round Blackstone's legs. He stroked it and it began to purr.

He said: "Of course, something went wrong. Something always does. A navvy known as Frying Pan Charlie got wind of the plot and peached. So you killed him."

"Did I?"

"You *borrowed* my pistol and shot him. Then you had his body dumped in the churchyard while the navvies were brawling. The law doesn't bother too much about navvies killed in brawls because you can never prove anything. There's a lot of loyalty among navvies."

Petro knocked out his pipe.

Blackstone said: "I don't think you knew who I was then." The realization pleased him because it meant the girl hadn't known to begin with. "So you thought it might be an idea to implicate me by using my gun. After all, you thought I was on the run. I wouldn't have stood much chance in court."

"Implicate," Petro said. "Such educated coves these Bow Street Runners."

"But you knew who I was by the time you suggested I might be able to join you. Someone had told you by then, Petro. Someone with good information. So you invited me to take part in the plot, taking care I didn't know any details until the last minute. So there I was with information from three sources that an attempt was going to be made to wreck the railway at Hartburn."

"And so you went there?" His anxiety wasn't disguised by his nonchalance.

"Oh yes," Blackstone said, "I went there all right."

Petro looked relieved.

Blackstone said: "So did Sir Richard Birnie, the chief Bow Street magistrate. So did a handful of constables and magistrates and two dozen Irish navigators from the other end of the line."

Petro relaxed.

"But I didn't stay," Blackstone said casually.

Petro stopped refilling his pipe. "Where did you go?"

The cat tried to jump on Blackstone's lap. "Where do you think? To the point where the robbery was to be staged."

"Then why haven't you got the money?"

"Ah," Blackstone said, "then you do agree there was going to be a robbery?" He turned to the girl. Molly, Polly, Dolly. He smiled at her, remembering the bruises on her face the first time they had met. "Did you know your king was a murderer?"

"I warned you against him," she said. "If you remember."

"I remember." The smell of honeysuckle, youth stunted and prematurely ageing.

"I told you not to go to Shanty Town."

Blackstone didn't ask why she had stayed with Petro. She wasn't the first girl he had met in the power of a bully. He pushed the cat away: it was black but he didn't know whose luck it represented.

"You made one mistake," Blackstone told the girl. "But you weren't to know. When we were at the fair in the village you told me you had been to see Petro the night before."

"Well?"

"Petro would hardly have asked you to stay that night."

"Why not?"

"Because," Blackstone said deliberately, "he was hoping to entertain another lady."

She frowned. "Who?"

"The missionary, Josephine Courtney. So, you see, I guessed you hadn't been to see him – you had it all rehearsed before."

She turned to Petro, letting the sheet fall from one breast. "Is that true?"

"Don't take any notice of him," Petro said. "He's trying to cause trouble between us. It's an old trick."

She covered herself again with the sheet. "Is it true, Rookie?"

"Blackie," he said.

"Is it true?"

"It's true enough. You've just got to decide who to believe."

Petro said: "Don't take any notice of this clever bastard." He stretched out a hand to touch her but she was too far away. "Can you imagine me going with a missionary."

"Or a missionary's sister," Blackstone said.

Petro frowned. "What are you babbling about now?"

"Her name isn't Courtney, it's Craig."

"So?"

"Perhaps you didn't even know her name," Blackstone said.

"I don't know what the hell you're talking about."

"I believe you. I'll have to jog your memory."

Blackstone recounted what Josephine Craig had told him. "You see, Petro, she came to Shanty Town to kill you."

"And why didn't she?"

"Because I said I'd do it for her."

Petro's hand tightened on his pipe. "You're mad."

"Just dedicated." Blackstone said to the girl: "You see, Molly, the man you're going with not only murders fellow navigators but he ravishes young girls." And kills small dogs, he thought. "If I give you the money will you go back to London? I'll see you get a decent job."

She looked at Petro. "Did you really have that missionary woman round to the cottage?"

Blackstone sighed. Murder and rape were of lesser importance than infidelity. "She isn't a missionary," he said. "She's a prater."

The girl said: "That's more your style, Petro."

"I didn't have her round," Petro said.

"He's telling the truth," Blackstone said. "She didn't go."

"How do you know?"

"Because," Blackstone said.

Petro yawned. "This is becoming boring. What happens now? You said you were going to kill me. Why don't you get on with it?"

Blackstone didn't think Birnie would take kindly to murder. Unless he killed Petro while he was trying to escape. But there was still the challenge.

"First," Blackstone said, "the test. All your bodyguards have a test, don't they, Petro, before they're taken on. A trial of strength or something. A spot of milling or wrestling. A dog fight, even."

"What do you suggest?"

"The traditional navvy fight – with shovels."

Petro grinned. "Have you ever had a spade fight?"

"No."

"I've seen a fair bit of claret tapped with shovels. And I've seen a few coves maimed for life. They're sharp, those spades – can take an arm off with a decent blow. Won't do these fine togs of yours much good, culley."

"Have you got a shovel?"

"Aye," Petro said. "In good repair, too, because I haven't used it much lately. Very sharp."

"In the field outside," Blackstone said. "I brought my shovel with me."

"Not blunt is it from all that navvying you've been doing?"

"It's as sharp as a razor." Blackstone turned to the girl. "You'd better get dressed."

He and Petro went down the stairs. For a moment Blackstone thought the dog was following him; but it was only the black cat.

The field was small with a docile horse in one corner; they led it into an orchard. The grass was dry and yellow and the hawthorn hedge was turning brown. The overhanging trees were hung with mauve plums and flushed apples. The smell of woodsmoke from a bonfire reached them.

Villagers gathered at the gate and around the hedge. Good witnesses for Birnie, Blackstone thought. He took off his coat and waistcoat and rolled up his sleeves. He left the pocket pistol under the coat, cocked. Petro's arms were brown, with biceps as thick as hams. Sunlight gleamed on his oiled hair.

"Any rules?" Petro asked. "Sometimes they have rules. Don't strike at a man when he's down. Three-minute rounds. That sort of thing."

"When did you ever take any notice of rules?" Blackstone picked up his shovel with its shiny, heart-shaped blade. "No rules – they're only made to be broken."

Petro shrugged. "Just as you please, culley. I've done some spading, you haven't. It's not like duelling, you know. No rapier thrust and parry. Nothing gentlemanly about it, Mr Blackstone."

In one corner of the field, near the gate leading to the road, Blackstone noticed a well with a handle, a wooden bucket and a lot of rope as if it were very deep.

"I'm ready," Blackstone said.

Around the gate the villagers took bets. Petro was clear favourite over the toff. Molly leaned against the gate, her face tense with worry for one of them.

Petro and Blackstone advanced into the middle of the field and faced each other. It was the sort of scene a Bow Street Runner should have broken up.

Petro fingered the blade of his shovel. It had hardly been used and it looked strong and bright. "On guard," he said suddenly, slashing at Blackstone's legs.

Blackstone, who had spent a lifetime with treachery, dodged.

"Just testing." Petro grinned.

Blackstone held the spade like a staff, right hand on the handle, left near the blade.

They circled each other while one of the villagers, the choir-master, shouted the odds. Petro was two to one on.

"Your move, culley," Petro said.

Blackstone watched Petro's eyes. And when he lunged swiftly and viciously he had already seen the blow coming. He leapt back; Petro advanced a couple of steps.

"Not an aggressive fighter, are you?" Petro said.

Blackstone cut upwards with the blade but Petro parried. Blade struck blade for the first time with a metallic crack.

Blackstone struck again. Again Petro took the blow with his shovel. For a moment they stood with weapons crossed. Petro pushed suddenly; Blackstone lost his footing and stumbled back. Petro leaped forward but he wasn't quick enough; Blackstone regained his footing and took the blow on the spade.

They paused. Blackstone listened to Petro's breathing: it was still controlled and even.

"Come on, culley," Petro said softly. "I want to do for you once and for all. Edmund Blackstone, Bow Street Runner." He spat on the grass. "I'll show your corpse to our missionary friend, our prater."

"It's your corpse she wants to see."

Petro feinted with his shovel; Blackstone waited. The afternoon was beginning to fade, the sun deepening as it found the evening mist.

Three times Petro feinted, then Blackstone went for him, thrusting, lunging, cutting – for Josephine Craig's sister, for the dog. But Petro side-stepped and Blackstone passed him. He turned as Petro came after him and they crossed spades again. Now both were breathing hungrily. Blackstone noticed that they were close to the well.

"Not bad," Petro grunted. "Not bad at all. But you haven't learned all the tricks, have you?"

As he spoke he kicked with his left foot. The boot cracked Blackstone's shin. Blackstone doubled up, hand instinctively reaching for the pain. Petro stepped back and slashed at him with the shovel; but the blow from the boot had made Blackstone stumble forward so that Petro over-reached himself, bringing the handle of his shovel on to Blackstone's shoulder. Pain flamed down his back and along his grazed arm.

Blackstone came up butting with his head, catching Petro in the belly. They retreated from each other, breath gasping. The villagers were silent as the men faced each other in the bronze light.

Petro didn't speak any more. His mouth was open, sweat trickled down his cheeks.

Blackstone said: "Perhaps you'd like a rest. Three-minute rounds." The grip of his wounded arm wasn't too strong. He wanted to end it quickly. He glanced round – down into the mouth of the well. He stepped sideways, accidentally kicking a pebble. It was a long time before the pebble hit water.

Petro heard it, too. He glanced towards the well and Blackstone knew they were thinking the same thing. Blackstone stepped forward jabbing with the point of the blade. Petro didn't react fast enough, blood appeared on his shirtfront.

"You bastard," Petro breathed. He swung, jabbed, clubbed. Blackstone fought him blow for blow. Once, Petro caught him on the chest with the edge of the blade, ripping open his shirt and cutting the flesh; he caught Petro in the face with the handle, shutting one eye.

They closed again a couple of feet from the edge of the well. Their shovels were crossed as they leaned against each other, half pushing, half leaning. No more talk. Sweat and blood mingling, bruises filling out.

They both exerted pressure at the same time. Tendons were standing out on Petro's neck. This was how he had got the authority – strength, bravery, brutality.

Something gave. For a fraction of a second Blackstone thought it was a bone breaking. But it was wood. The shaft of his shovel snapped with a crack so that he was left with the handle in one hand, the blade in the other, the shaft of Petro's shovel hard against his throat.

Blackstone choked, dropped the handle and clawed at Petro's shaft. Petro shoved forward, Blackstone stepped back. One foot from the edge of the well.

"Got you, culley," Petro said.

He thrust at Blackstone's neck with the shaft. Blackstone coughed and clawed; he had to escape from the pressure; he stepped back with one foot but there was nothing beneath it – nothing for a long way down.

He glanced down. Dry moss on the walls, then unfathomable darkness.

He thrust his leg farther back so that it reached the wall on the other side and he was spanning the side of the mouth of the well. To make him plunge down Petro would either have to dislodge his front foot or push him sideways.

Petro put one foot on the edge of the well. Blackstone held the blade of his shovel in one hand. He relaxed as Petro shoved forward and managed to get both feet on the far side of the well.

As he swayed on the ledge he hit Petro on the side of the head with the flat of the blade and threw himself backwards. As he fell he heard Petro scream.

All he could see was the handle rotating and the rope spinning. He jumped for the handle and tried to hold it. But it jumped free. He shouted to the villagers to help him.

They ran across the field and held the handle. Blackstone peered down. He could see Petro hanging on to the bucket. The rope was frayed in places.

He shouted down the well-shaft to Petro to hold on. His voice echoed a couple of times before sinking in the water. Petro's body swung like a pendulum.

They began to turn the handle with strands of rope snapping as the lifeline re-wound itself. They saw Petro's hands and the top of his head.

From the well-shaft came Petro's voice. "I can't hang on any longer."

"Another minute," Blackstone shouted. "Hang on another minute." Why, he didn't know.

First his hands appeared, grazed and shining white. Then the top of his head. Blackstone grabbed one wrist, the choir-master the other.

They dropped him on the grass where he lay shivering, his fingers locked as though still gripping the rope. After a while the hands relaxed and Petro turned on his back to gaze at the darkening sky. "Why?" he asked. "Why?"

Blackstone fingered his bruised windpipe. "Because I didn't want to be accused of murder."

"But you said you'd kill me."

"Maybe I will," Blackstone said. "The legal way. I'm arresting you, Petro, and bringing charges against you that could take you to the gallows."

"No proof," Petro said. His voice was weak. "Used your pistol."

Blackstone shook his head. "Not Frying Pan. I'm charging you with assaulting a young girl by the name of Mary Craig. I shouldn't have much difficulty in proving it, Petro. And that sort of assault is a hanging job."

The girl stood at the gate. She didn't move as the two of them passed her, Blackstone's pistol in Petro's back. Blackstone found some sovereigns in his coat pocket. He gave them to her and said: "Take my advice. Go back to London. I'll get you a job."

She threw the sovereigns in the dust. "Keep your charity," she said.

"We were going back together once."

"You cheated."

"And you didn't?"

"If you'd have got the reward I'd have gone with you. I couldn't help it about Petro. I was scared of him. But I'd have gone with you."

"Go now then."

"No Rookie." Her voice, her expression, were the same as they had been that first day in The Naked Man. "Things are different now. I thought we were on the same side. I'd have gone with Rookie but not Edmund Blackstone."

She walked down the road leaving the coins in the dust. Blackstone picked them up and gave them to the villagers. After all, most of them had lost money on him.

CHAPTER THREE

Dawn on 27 September 1825. The fields were clean with dew and mist was still trapped in the hollows. But it was going to be a fine day because England was becalmed in fine weather.

Already spectators were lining the track. From a distance they looked like insects clinging to a length of wire.

They were beginning to occupy the fields, too, arriving on horseback, in gigs, coaches-and-four, donkey carts, on foot. They brought children and dogs and victuals; and with them came the villains. Blackstone didn't recognize them, merely identified their calling – pickpockets with their stickmen, speelers, thimble-riggers, a kidsman or two, gonophs, broadsmen, mudlarks who had taken to the dust – Blackstone had seen them all at prizefights, race meetings, cricket matches. Ballad sheets about the railway were selling for a halfpenny and the warm smell from the loaves on sale at the roadside – along with ham, cheese and pickles – made the fresh morning air cosy.

The biggest crowds were gathered on the sloping fields around Brussleton where a stationary engine had to haul the coal wagons to the top. "They want to see the wagons hit the bottom," Blackstone told Josephine Craig, who was holding his arm. She looked very elegant and composed, in a blue silk dress, with a darker blue bonnet and a parasol;

her face was more gentle, her bearing more feminine than it had been before.

"Why were you distributing those handbills?" he asked.

"They paid me," she said. "I needed money. In any case, I hated the railways and anything connected with them."

"Who paid you?"

"Oh, the anti-railway groups. They don't make any secret of it, do they?"

"I think," Blackstone said, "that your last rash of handbills may have been breaking the law. Incitement to riot or something like that."

"Are you going to prosecute?"

"Not if you behave yourself," Blackstone told her.

They climbed out of their carriage and walked across the fields to Shildon where Locomotion was waiting.

She said: "What will happen to Petro?"

"He'll be hanged," Blackstone said. "You'll have to give evidence. And your sister, I'm afraid. The two navvies who were with him that day were two of his bodyguards. They'll give evidence against him – I've seen to that."

"It doesn't seem to matter so much any more."

"Think of your sister," Blackstone said. "Then it matters."

"Yes," she said, "then it matters."

At Shildon they met George Stephenson and his brother James. None of the Peases were present because there had been a death in the family; Eccleston was waiting at the Stockton end.

George Stephenson took Blackstone aside. "Are you sure everything's going to be all right?"

"Don't worry," Blackstone said.

"If the navvies don't get paid they'll wreck the line."

"They're getting paid. Fighting Cocks as arranged."

They walked round Locomotion, as jaunty as ever this

burgeoning morning. "Everything's been taken care of and no one except the privileged few will ever know about the robbery – or how easy it is to rob a train." Blackstone counted on his fingers. "Who knows anyway? You and your brother James so that's all right. Gowland, the fireman, who's agreed not to talk. Eccleston and the rest of the committee. They've all agreed to forget it in their own interests."

Stephenson said: "What about the two guards looking after the bags?"

"Villains," Blackstone told him. "Both in Challoner's pay. That's why they couldn't shoot straight when Challoner and his accomplice arrived. They're not likely to talk. Nor is Challoner. Nor is the fellow who fell off the train with brother James and ran for it. Jonathan Smiles is quite happy with his horses and his sovereigns and Petro isn't likely to involve himself in a train robbery as well as rape and I've spoken to his bodyguards. You see," Blackstone explained, "they're giving evidence against him and they're not being charged. So you've got no worries." He touched the engine's smokestack; half way up there was a small dent where a bullet had struck it. "No worries except the engine. Is it all right?"

Stephenson nodded. "As far as I know. She couldn't have had a tougher trial than she had yesterday." He tapped the wheels with his cane. "I'm a bit worried about those. And I'm a bit worried about the load she's got to pull. I may have overdone it. The whole train will be four hundred feet long and we've issued tickets to three hundred passengers. But there are going to be more. Many more." Stephenson gazed at the crowds along the line. "God knows what the weight will be."

"Locomotion looks strong enough."

Stephenson took his arm. "I hope so, lad. I hope so." He frowned, pushing his big black eyebrows together. "I wonder if you have any idea what this means to me?"

Blackstone thought he did.

"It means everything. It means all my past and all my future." His accent thickened. "I don't really know which is the more important." He led Blackstone alongside the train. "I suppose you know they tried to make a fool of me in London."

"I know they *tried*."

"Tried and succeeded. We've got to show them today, lad. If we don't, the enemies of progress have won the day."

"You'll show them," Blackstone said.

They stopped beside the first railway passenger coach, the Experiment. It had been delivered the day before and it looked like a stagecoach mounted on an unsprung frame. The seats were cushioned and there was a carpet and a table for the directors riding to Stockton.

"What do you think of it?" Stephenson asked.

Blackstone, who didn't think much of it, said: "I suppose it serves its purpose. It looks too much like an adaptation of road transport – a concession."

"I know what you mean. We'll have proper coaches soon. Railway coaches." They walked back. "Where's Birnie this morning?"

"Waiting at the Stockton end," Blackstone said.

But he wasn't. He was standing beside the engine talking to Josephine Craig.

"A word in your ear," Birnie said.

Blackstone glanced at his Breguet. "The train's about to start, sir. An historic moment."

Birnie took his arm. "Just what the hell is going on, Blackstone? Why did you leave me at Hartburn? What happened to the money and what's all this I hear about a fight with shovels?"

"It will take a long time to explain...."

"I'm sure it will. I warned you about your vendetta with Challoner."

The directors were climbing into Experiment. "I believe they have a place reserved for you, sir. I should take it now if I were you...."

Birnie glanced at the coach. "I want an explanation, Blackstone."

"Very well," Blackstone began. Then he said: "I believe someone's taking your place, sir...."

Birnie swore a rare oath. "I'll meet you at Stockton, Blackstone. Your explanation will have to be masterly. If it doesn't satisfy me then I shall take your baton away from you. Is that understood?"

"Understood," Blackstone said. Understood but not accepted. He helped the black-clothed figure into the coach. The directors were already reaching for their hip flasks to prepare themselves for the historic journey; pride and apprehension fighting each other on their faces.

"Bon voyage," Blackstone said. "I hope the boiler doesn't blow up."

Birnie didn't reply.

Ten wagons loaded with coal were hauled by horses from the Phoenix pit at Witton Park to the bottom of the slope at Etherley. There they were attached to thick hempen rope and pulled to the top by the stationary engine.

From the top they ran to the other side under their own volition. At the bottom another wagon loaded with flour was attached and horses drew the seven wagons over the Gaunless iron bridge to the bottom of the slope at Brussleton.

In the crowds, laying thick on the fields, there was a movement, like the first eddy on a calm sea before a storm. The eddy reached the track and spread across it. The young lads went first, then the men; within seconds the S and D's first known passengers were on board, sitting on coal and flour.

The 60hp beam engine at the top of Brussleton Bank started up. The silence in the fields was complete, as if an anthem were being played; eating, guzzling, suckling, singing, stopped and the pickpockets' fingers froze in their victims' pockets.

The rope tightened. The wagons ascended at 8mph, spilling a few passengers, then made their way down the other side to meet Locomotion waiting with Experiment and twenty-one new coal wagons fitted with seats.

Blackstone and Josephine Craig sat in one of the new wagons. Blackstone shielded her as, with a great cheer, the crowd stormed the train; the silk of her dress was slippery to the touch and he could feel her warmth beneath it; he shielded her more protectively. They were squeezed into the side of the wagon with men and women standing on their feet and a boy with red hair staring at them, eyes on the same level as theirs. Here and there Blackstone noticed railway officials wearing blue sashes asking for tickets; but there weren't many of them and they soon submerged. The boy, who smelled of peppermint, continued to stare.

"We'll never get going with all these people," Josephine said.

"Stephenson will do it," Blackstone said. "Locomotion will do it."

Locomotion answered with a roar of steam. Women screamed and fainted and some of the passengers took to the fields.

Blackstone didn't move. Nor did the red-haired boy.

Josephine said: "You're very calm."

"It's only the safety valve lifting."

"You know a lot about these puffing Billies."

"So do you," Blackstone reminded her. "They make cows run dry and women miscarry."

The driver and his mate – George and James Stephenson – stayed put and the uninvited passengers returned.

George Stephenson opened the regulator and Locomotion inched forward, preceded by a horseman carrying a banner in Latin – "Through private danger to the public good". Fitting, Blackstone thought.

Smoke and cinders flew, pistons thumped and a few hundred yards along the track a wagon reserved for engineers and surveyors came off the rails.

"Perhaps," Josephine said, "my handbills won't be necessary."

"It's nothing," Blackstone said.

Shouting and instructing each other, the passengers put the wagon back on the rails. Locomotion moved forward and the wagon came off again.

Stephenson jumped from the platform to inspect it. "A wheel's shifted off the axle," he said. "We'll have to leave it at the next loop."

The "procession of wagons", as the programme described it, made Sim Pasture before the next breakdown. This time it was the engine.

George and his brother went to work behind a veil of steam. "Like I said," said the red-haired boy's father, "the engine will never answer."

"She's answered already," Blackstone said.

"You'll see," the man said.

Stephenson climbed on to the platform and announced that a piece of oakum had interfered with one of the valves on the feed pump. "Nothing to worry about," he shouted.

"We'll see," the boy's father said.

Horsemen riding beside the train shouted challenges and George Stephenson told the man with the banner to get out of the way. "I'm game if you are," he shouted.

The "procession" rattled and swayed for 8½ miles, reaching the junction with the Darlington line at noon. The horsemen were far behind.

More than 10,000 spectators were waiting to welcome Locomotion. The six wagons loaded with coal were detached and the contents distributed; two more wagons were attached, one containing dignitaries from Darlington, the other the Yarm town band.

Locomotion got under way again on the last, five-mile stretch to Stockton, stopping at Goosepool for water.

"She'll never make it," the boy's father said.

"Would you care to make a wager?" Blackstone asked.

"I'm not a betting man," the man said.

Near Whiteley Springs the track ran beside the road. Coachmen whipped up their horses to try to keep up with the wild travelling engine but soon railway and road went their separate ways.

At 3.45pm – three-quarters of an hour late – Locomotion and her train passed over St John's crossing on to Stockton Quay. There were forty thousand waiting for her.

"Pity you're not a betting man," Blackstone said to the boy's father.

"Don't believe in it," the man said.

Blackstone helped Josephine on to the quay.

Seven eighteen-pound cannons fired a salute, a band on the quay and the Yarm town band on the train played "God Save the King", church bells peeled.

Blackstone saw Birnie thrusting his way through the cheering crowd. He made hasty arrangements with Josephine to meet her later in a coffee house and escaped. There was one more conspirator to see.

Sir Joshua Eccleston was surprised. He was standing in front of the mirror in his hotel room knotting his white tie for the banquet that evening.

Blackstone walked in without knocking. "Good evening," he said. He sat down on a chair beside the bed, one hand on the pistol in his pocket.

"What the devil are you doing here?"

"My job," Blackstone said.

"As I understand it, you failed in your job – the money was stolen."

"Was it? Then can you explain to me how the navvies – and everyone else – were paid this afternoon?"

"They can't have been...." Eccleston began. In the candle-light his pulpit face was cunning.

"Why not? Because Challoner's got the blunt and is going to hand it over to you when he's taken his cut."

"You'd better get out," Eccleston said. "You seem to have taken leave of your senses."

"Better men than you have said that to me, Sir Joshua."

"I'll call the management."

"I'll do it if you like." Blackstone reached for the bell-rope behind the bed.

Eccleston raised his hand. "Don't bother. Just tell me what you're raving about and then get out. I shall see Birnie about this tonight."

"You will indeed," Blackstone told him. He fingered the pistol as Eccleston sat down on the dressing-table stool.

"What's this about the navvies being paid?"

"Just that," Blackstone said. "They were paid. And I'm told they're having a fine old randy already fighting the Irish. They'll enjoy that. So will the Irish."

Eccleston said: "I don't understand. I thought the thieves got clean away with the two leather bags."

"They did," Blackstone said. "Challoner got clean away with two leather bags filled with bullets which I made during my navvying days and copies of a publication called *The Navigator*. I hope he reads *The Navigator* – there's a lot of good advice in it for him. Then he can shoot himself with one of my bullets."

Blackstone took some snuff with his free hand. "I'll explain," he went on. "It didn't occur to me for a long time, then a few things began to fit into place. To start with, *you* didn't call in Bow Street, did you, Sir Joshua? We were the last people you wanted on the scene. It was George Stephenson who did that – good old George. What you were doing, of course, was robbing yourself – not a very difficult task when you know exactly when each delivery of wages is going to be moved. But I'll give you one thing, Sir Joshua, you employed the best – you employed Challoner."

Blackstone watched Eccleston's hand moving towards a drawer in the dressing-table. "So there you were. One robbery successfully completed. Another planned with a final spectacular coup. Then Bow Street was called in and you and Challoner had to do a bit of re-thinking. But you adapted very well. You, Challoner and Hawkins."

"Hawkins?" Eccleston's voice had lost its ring. "He's against everything I stand for."

"Maybe he is," Blackstone said. "But you can't afford to stand by your principles – railways, progress, all that sort of thing – when you're facing bankruptcy, ruin."

"Who's facing ruin?"

"You are. More than ever at this moment." He saw muscles moving in Eccleston's jaw. He went on: "I don't know who made the first approach. You, I suppose, as you were broke. Anyway, you and Hawkins got together. Hawkins and his cronies had virtually lost the battle of the S and D. The only thing that could save them would be a spectacular disaster. So together you planned a couple of robberies which would make the navvies, incited by Petro, fighting mad. If they hadn't got their money today God knows what would have happened. Petro could have got them to pull up the line, blow up the bridges, blow up Locomotion. And you" – Blackstone wagged his finger – "would have got the swag because Hawkins isn't interested in money – he's got enough."

Eccleston fiddled with his tie; it was beautifully knotted, Blackstone noted.

Blackstone said: "As I say, you adapted very well to Bow Street. You cancelled the second highway robbery just in case anything went wrong. All that remained was the master stroke – moving the money by train, without letting Bow Street know. Faster, neater. A flamboyant touch, too, ringing with sincerity – show the world that the railways are safe. In fact you were setting out to do the very reverse." Blackstone improvised. "Challoner was in favour of the train, too. He's a vain man – all criminals are. He wanted to make criminal history – the first train robbery. He did in a way – the first unsuccessful one."

"I think you're quite mad," Eccleston said.

"Is that why you're reaching for that gun?"

Blackstone dived across the room and slammed the drawer on Eccleston's fingers. Eccleston screamed. "Now," Blackstone said, "let's see, shall we?" He opened the drawer; inside was a small, double-barrelled tap-action pocket pistol. "By Ketland, I think," Blackstone said. He dropped it into his pocket. Then sat down again facing Eccleston. "Do you know when I first began to suspect you?" he asked.

Eccleston didn't reply.

"When I first discovered that Challoner, and presumably Petro and Pascoe, knew that I was disguised as a navvy." Blackstone leaned forward. "Only one person could have told them. There were four of us at your house that day – Stephenson, Birnie, you and me. It wasn't Stephenson – that would be ludicrous – and, in any case, he called in Bow Street. So that left you. I then got someone to check on you in Liverpool. A contact of mine who has a way with safes. He discovered you were broke, Sir Joshua. A desperate man. What better way of becoming solvent again than to rob yourself? – or get someone to do it for you. The first robbery was covered by insurance. Right?"

"It's no secret," Eccleston murmured.

"So that was money in your pocket on top of the swag after you'd given Challoner his share and handed out a few sovereigns to Petro and his accomplices. Navvies come pretty cheap, don't they, Eccleston?"

"Do they?"

"So that left the last big robbery. A lot of brass involved in this one. Just half would be enough to keep a man in home comforts for the rest of his life. Of course the money would have to be replaced and I doubt if the insurance company would cough up as easily this time, if at all. But that wouldn't have bothered you, would it, Sir Joshua, because you would have been well away by then? Where were you meeting him, Manchester?"

"I'm going to call the manager," Eccleston said.

"First let me finish. On the day before the robbery I went to Darlington. I saw a magistrate and a constable and we went round to your offices. We found an ambitious scheme afoot – transferring cash by the new railway, taking it first to Shildon. Your staff were quite enthusiastic because Sir Joshua himself had suggested it. Carrying a fortune the whole length of the railway. Marvellous boost for steam locomotion – all that sort of thing. But you'd intended it that way for a long time. So, with the approval of the magistrate and the constable – Bow Street still carries considerable weight whatever Peel may have you believe – I arranged a substitution. I put the bullets and the handbills in the leather bags and moved the cash by stagecoach. Your staff were sworn to secrecy – even from you. That's how the navvies got paid and are now happily fighting it out with the Irish."

"You can't prove any of it," Eccleston said.

"You know," Blackstone said, "I've heard many men say that. They're now either in Van Diemen's Land, on the hulks, or dead. In fact," he went on, "I've got rather a good case. Your financial state. The sum of £3,000 paid into a private account in Liverpool just after the first robbery. Statements from Petro and Pascoe implicating you. And this." He tossed a ticket on the bed. "A booking made by you on the midnight coach tonight for Manchester. An odd journey to take at the height of the celebrations? On top of that, I'm quite sure Sir Geoffrey Hawkins would be happy to give evidence against you."

Eccleston broke. "I can tell you where you can find Challoner. You want him, don't you, Blackstone?"

"Not particularly," Blackstone lied. "In any case he won't hang around Manchester when he finds he's got a lot of bullets and religious tracts for his pains." Blackstone stood up.

"Now we have to go and see Birnie. Then a magistrate. It's a pity you decided to stay too long in Stockton. Why was that, Sir Joshua? Had you prepared an after-dinner speech?"

Birnie said: "It's all been most unorthodox, Blackstone. Most unorthodox."

They were standing in an ante-room of the Town Hall. The banquet was nearing an end and there had been twenty-three toasts to George Stephenson.

"May I suggest," Blackstone said, "that it only seemed unorthodox because you were too close to the case?"

Birnie's head bobbed like a marionette's above his stiff white collar and boiled shirt. "At least the railway's safe," he admitted. "And the future of the railways." He smiled, which made Blackstone suspect that he had been drinking. "Anyway, you seem to have broken your run of failures."

"Thank you, sir."

"Except that you lost Challoner."

"I'll get him one day," Blackstone said.

"I wonder." Birnie peered at Blackstone. "I wonder if you really want to." He walked out of the room, marionetted head shaking.

Josephine Craig was waiting in the corridor outside. "So it's all over?" she said.

"Yes," Blackstone said, "it's all over."

"Now what?" Her eyes were moist.

"I think," he said, "that Bow Street could do with a missionary." He kissed her and offered her his arm. Remembering the navvies' wedding ceremony he took care to step around the cleaner's broom which had fallen across the corridor.

HISTORICAL NOTE

Locomotion broke a wheel within a week of her maiden journey. Within two years she was fitted with a complete set of wheels of a different type. Within three years she burst her boiler. She was in service on the Stockton and Darlington until 1840. After that she was not used until the opening of the Redcar line in June 1846. In 1850 she was sold to the Pease family and used for water-pumping in a colliery. In 1857 she was presented to the S and D by the Peases to be preserved. She was first put on show at North Road Station, Darlington, and then, in April 1892, transferred to the main line station at Bank Top, Darlington.

Printed in Great Britain
by Amazon